Mystery on Mount Dusk

by

Aleah Taylor

Neverland Publishing Company
Miami, FL

Copyright © 2015 by Aleah Taylor

Cover Design by Cary Polkovitz

Library of Congress Control Number: 2015911456

Printed in the United States of America

ISBN: 978-0-9965595-1-5

www.neverlandpublishing.com

Dedicated with all of my love to my dearest son Tommi who inspired so much of this book.

CHAPTER 1

Packing Up

*T*en year old George Mutton glanced around at his bedroom for the last time. He looked at all of the stains on the carpet, monuments to particularly funny mischief on his behalf. He viewed the deep cuts in the wall that marked his wonderful idea of self-expression with a pair of scissors (George's right buttock had never quite felt the same after his mother had gotten through with him).

George was moving house—well, not just moving house—moving to a whole new town with a new cold climate. The big move had been inspired by his mother's recent discovery that she was pregnant. As it turns out, George's mother was pregnant with twins and, during one particularly stressful morning when George's mother had discovered that she would now need more bedrooms, she promptly put their house up for sale and decided that she needed to live in a quiet town to cope with the two new arrivals. The quiet town she chose was the town of Mount Dusk. From what George had gathered by eavesdropping on his parents, it was a town comprising fifty inhabitants, fifteen of which were under the age of seventeen, and was located at the top of a mountain, bringing the ideal isolation that Mrs. Mutton desired.

George didn't mind the idea of moving too much; he would miss his friends, but, then again, he was certain that there would be more adventure for him living on top of a mountain than there would be in the suburbs where he grew up. George despised the suburbs; to him there could be nothing more boring. The biggest news in his suburb this year had been Mrs. Anderson's blocked toilet. No, George did not find moving towns hard to deal with. George's seven-year-old sister Maggie, on the other hand, was a different story. Maggie had cried, held her breath, threatened to run away, called Grandma to screech stories of imaginary abuse and supposed kidnap, and that was only within the first twenty-four hours of finding out about the move. Since then, she had tried her hardest to protest the move by not speaking to Mr. and Mrs. Mutton. Instead of verbal communication, Maggie decided that she was going to communicate using a mixture of scathing looks and loud sniffs from her little nose above a dramatically quivering lip.

George took one last sweeping look of the bedroom, catching a glimpse of himself in his old cracked mirror. His light brown hair, freshly cut by his mother, was short and bristly; his light blue eyes portrayed a hint of sadness at leaving his old room behind. He quickly smiled at his reflection, as if trying to reassure himself, and then left the room to carry the last of his bags outside to the family's old station wagon. Mr. Mutton was talking to the removalist, trying, and failing dismally, to navigate the two men carrying the Mutton family's refrigerator.

"Left, sorry, right! Whoops! So sorry, dear man, it was left. Not to worry. I'm sure my wife Carol can patch up that leg, I've always said they make gutters too high."

George turned away and laughed; his dad was the klutz of the family. It was a trait that saw his mother constantly chasing Mr. Mutton with a string of exasperated reprimands.

"Oh, Larry, let the men do their job. For Pete's sake!" Mrs. Mutton cried as her husband tripped and rammed into the back of a rather burly removalist.

Mrs. Mutton looked very harassed. "George, dear," she called, "Go and check on your sister. I haven't seen her for a while...poor dear." She then bustled away, a worried look crossing her round features.

George sighed and slowly ambled back across the front yard. George did not want to check on his sister; as far as he was concerned she was a spoilt brat. Everyone else had to help with the packing and the moving but, oh no, not the poor little princess. She could just spill out a few tears and hide in a corner somewhere until all the work was done for her. George walked through the house to the pink bedroom at the end of the hallway.

"Maggie," he called. "Don't worry. The work's done; you can re-surface again."

He found his sister tucked into a ball in the corner of her bedroom.

"G...go away!" She choked at him, tears streaming down her small face. "I don't want to talk to you...you don't even care!"

George rolled his eyes and slumped down next to her, feeling his annoyance slipping into pity despite himself.

"Oh, come on, Maggie. It really isn't that bad. At least you get all new furniture...I don't."

Maggie gave a dark, mirthless laugh. "Ha, oh yeah, whoop-dee-doo! 'Here, Maggie, you lose all of your friends and memories, but there you go, have a bookshelf.'"

George looked down at the little ball with messy dark brown hair that was his sister. For the life of him he couldn't see what the big loss was but he put his arm around her anyway.

"Well, if it's any consolation, I'll spend more time with you until you get new friends."

Sure that he had said something reassuring, he gave his

sister a grin. Instead of grinning back, Maggie gave him a look of deepest loathing.

"I don't want new friends!" she screeched at him and then ran out of the room sobbing harder than ever.

$$\mathcal{XXX}$$

Two hours later the whole family was finally packed into the car, each cradling a breakable something that Mrs. Mutton hadn't entrusted to the removalists.

"Who knows with those men," she had clucked to herself, thrusting vases into everyone's lap. "They didn't even blink when they saw the antiques. Imagine that!"

When they finally drove past the end of suburbia George's stomach did a little back flip. *A new home*, George thought to himself, *and in the mountains! I can't wait to see it.* George pictured a tiny town nestled on the top of a mountain, encircled with mist. Little cottages with inhabitants shunned from the city, mystery seeping out from under every door. George grinned. Although it was probably just a normal town, he couldn't help but dream because that's just what George did; everything was potentially exciting to George. And with these enticing images buzzing around in his mind he drifted slowly to sleep.

"George, George sweetheart, we're here."

George jerked awake at the sound of his mother's voice. As soon as his tired and foggy mind grasped what his mother had just said he wound down the car window and stuck his head out. What he saw was a long street of tiny stone cottages with chimneys breathing smoke into the frosty sky, and, above the street, towering over its inhabitants was the peak of Mount Dusk. Huge boulders and rough green foliage, packed so close together it looked like one giant shrub. The sky above was a sinister mass of swirling grey, giving the town a drained, shadowy quality. George grinned. In his opinion the town was perfect, it

4

looked mysterious and wild; it was George's kind of town indeed. George turned to his little sister, his face still lit up with excitement, but Maggie did not look excited—she looked anything but. Her mouth was hanging open in apparent disgust, her eyes were brimming with tears and her hands clutched at the car door, it seemed, for support.

"This is it? How is this even a town?" Maggie whispered to herself in a choked, high-pitched voice.

Mrs. Mutton turned in her seat, the expression on her face mirroring George's. But, at the sight of her daughter's displeasure, her smile sagged a little and concern flickered in her deep blue eyes.

"It's fantastic, Mum!" George exclaimed, angry at Maggie for tainting their mother's happiness.

Mrs. Mutton gave him an appreciative smile and turned back around in her seat with a small, disappointed sigh.

Stupid Maggie, thought George savagely. *She could at least act happy but, no, that would take a personality transplant.* George glared at his sister as she turned to face him.

"Oh, come on," she said. "You can't actually like this ridiculous place?"

George leaned over to her and replied in a hiss.

"I do, you see. I'm just happy that Mum's happy. Apparently, though, you don't care at all."

Maggie narrowed her eyes but seemingly had no retort because she turned back to stare glumly out of the window again.

The Mutton family trundled down the rickety street in search of their new house.

"Now, the real estate agent said it was number fifty-six Clover place. Look out for it, kids!"

George looked eagerly out of the window and started trying to find the house numbers on the little stone mail boxes that sat guard at the front of every garden. *Fifty two...fifty four...fifty six!*

"This is it!" Mrs. Mutton exclaimed, sitting up as straight as she could with her big pregnant belly fighting for room with the seat belt.

The Mutton family's new residence was a large, one level stone cottage. The front garden held all sorts of plants, from delicate little flowers to big tough looking shrubs. The large gates into the back garden at the end of the driveway were made of twisting wrought iron hidden by intricately entwined vines that had sneakily crept along the roof to claim the small stone chimney too. The windows of the house were tall and arched at the top and the double front doors were huge and made of oak. George could not believe his luck! It was the best house he'd ever seen! It looked creepy, comfortable and obviously had some form of history that George could daydream about. Beside George, Maggie was hissing a stream of very bad language under her breath.

"Well what do you think?" Mr. Mutton asked, turning around in his seat and grinning.

"Awesome!" George said at once, eyes bright with anticipation.

"Humph," Maggie muttered.

The Mutton family climbed out of the car, each carrying one of the "special-somethings" that Mrs. Mutton had only entrusted to their laps. George and Mr. Mutton ran ahead, Mr. Mutton fumbled with the house keys, muttering;

"Laundry door key...no...back door...no...laundry again...ah."

Mr. Mutton slotted the correct front door key into the lock and turned it. The lock gave a momentous click and then the door was opened by one of Mr. Mutton's flailing limbs as he stumbled over the threshold.

George stepped into the house. The sweet smell of mold hit his nostrils, reminding him of some particularly old library books he had borrowed once. The ceiling was wooden and stained to be a deep brown, the floors were the same. George had the momentary feeling that he had just climbed into a fancy tree until he saw something very unlike the inside of a tree.

Stained glass windows lined the long hallway and from the look of them they were beautiful portraits of a family.

George concluded that this cottage must have once belonged to a family through many generations as there were many windows. George meandered slowly down the long hallway looking at them in detail. The first two windows were of a man and woman who looked to be husband and wife. Their hands reached out towards each other as if each was trying to get into the other's picture. The two windows on the opposite wall facing this couple were of two young girls who were identical. They were curtsying.

George decided that these girls must be their children. A space separated this window family from their neighbors then followed what seemed to be another married couple's pictures. Both looked rather regal and somber with only one children's window facing them. A sullen looking little boy stared dully out at his parents. George studied the boy and realized that he actually looked slightly angry. After another space, George found the last window family. The couple in this group looked incredibly sad; their heads were bowed and glass tears slipped from their eyes. The two children facing them were of the same effect, silently crying forever more. They were two girls, one slightly taller and darker than her little blonde sister. George turned and ran back up the hallway to tell the rest of his family about the strange windows. He found his mother, father and sister standing in the lounge room studying the curtains. Why were his family so interested in the drapes? George joined them and, on closer inspection, discovered that the curtains were covered in a family tree woven into the fabric.

"Oh, this is so interesting!" Mrs. Mutton cried tracing a short finger over one of the names: *Thomas Regale*.

Even Maggie looked slightly interested, or at least did not seem to be complaining. George quickly explained about the hallway and the Mutton family trooped down to see the mysterious windows for themselves.

"Goodness!" Mrs. Mutton exclaimed, catching sight of the crying couple down the end. "The real estate agent never mentioned that these were here!"

Mrs. Mutton turned to look at her husband with a slightly accusing stare as if he too had failed to tell her about the windows.

"Yes, bit personal isn't it...you'd think they would have taken these out before selling the house, but still...interesting," Mr. Mutton mumbled almost to himself, rubbing a long-fingered hand over his knobbly chin.

Normally, George would have been excited at an unknown-something to investigate, but George felt strange about these windows. There was something unnerving about this family. The windows almost seemed like a warning, from a happy family...to a sad family and for once George was hesitant to discover just what this warning was about.

xxx

The next few days following their move to Mount Dusk were very chaotic for the Mutton family. Mr. Mutton had gotten thoroughly banged up after trying to help the removalists lift every little thing into the new house.

"I've lived with this lounge for ten years and I swear it was never this heavy—oh well, toes heal!"

Mrs. Mutton spent a lot of time clucking her tongue and shunting vases around the place then standing back to see their effect. Maggie had screamed and bawled to get a bigger bedroom than George, not without success, and spent the next couple of days dropping hints that George's room resembled a mouse hole.

George liked his bedroom. Although it was indeed the smallest room in the house it was also the oddest—a complete circle at the end of the house with leaf shapes carved all over the roof. At first George thought that the ceiling looked a bit too

8

girly, but on closer inspection he discovered that tiny names had been engraved inside the little leaves, which satisfied his curiosity and made him forget about being girly. The round walls were lined with thick dark blue curtains that gave the room a very cozy feel and George had felt completely comfortable there drifting asleep, even on his first night. Maggie on the other hand had slept in Mr. and Mrs. Mutton's bed, giving George sufficient cause to tease her the next day about being a big baby.

In the suburbs, the Mutton's backyard had been a complete square with only pretty little poppies in a straight line across the back for a bit of color. This new backyard, however, was full of plants twisting this way and that, the grass barely noticeable through the intertwining rebel branches. George examined the garden for a long time, continually finding little spiders scurrying away from his footsteps. Now this was George's style!

xxx

George and Maggie were to start school the next morning. George was a little apprehensive; he had never been the "new kid" before and wasn't sure what the other students would be like. George pictured the school to be tiny as there were only fifteen students in it, seventeen including George and Maggie. This made George think that, if ten did not like him, he'd only have five people with which to make friends. But as much as George was nervous he was also excited. It was, after all, an adventure.

The two Mutton children accompanied their mother to shop for school supplies at the cluster of little shops near the base of Mount Dusk. They picked up all of the usual pens and pencils, exercise books and school uniforms but they also had to buy a book each called *The Mysterious Mount Dusk*.

George wanted to read the book straight away, to see what

was so mysterious, but Mrs. Mutton insisted on the children ironing their uniforms for the next day and trying them on for her. The uniforms were black with the school's emblem on the back in glittering white. Maggie wore a long, thick skirt and a long sleeved button up shirt, while George wore dressy black trousers and a black shirt with a white tie.

"Oh, don't you both just look gorgeous!" Mrs. Mutton beamed, fussing around them and picking at pieces of stray lint.

"Gorgeous?" spat Maggie. "We could be going to a funeral in all this black!"

"Well, it looks very smart to me," concluded Mrs. Mutton, as she ushered them into their rooms to change and go to sleep ready for their very first day at Mount Dusk Academy.

CHAPTER 2

Mount Dusk Academy

Mr. Mutton drove George and Maggie to school the next day on his way to work. Mr. Mutton had gotten a job as a local carpenter almost as soon as he had arrived and was very excited himself. It was his first day, too.

"See ya, kids!" He boomed. "Wish me luck and good luck to you both."

"Good luck, Dad," George replied, "and...be careful with your tools."

George and Maggie clambered out of the car and faced their new school. The sloping lawns at the front were a lush green surrounded by rocky, rugged terrain. The school itself was huge. George had been picturing a tiny little stone cottage, but Mount Dusk Academy was certainly no cottage. It rose in graceful towers on both sides of the building and the front gates were ridiculously tall and made of brass. It was an old castle! The windows were tall and elegant and the roof peaked to a sharp point in the middle.

George and Maggie walked up to the front gates and, once they had entered, they stopped and looked at the beautiful garden in front of them. Vibrant pinks, yellows, blues, purples and reds hit their eyes as they studied the huge mass of flowers.

Garden seats had been placed in the flower beds and they were brass too. The overall effect was stunning. Maggie's face, which had been tense and sulky in the car, now lit up in delight as she ran to the winding paths through the flowers. George sat on a bench to watch his sister. He did not want to leave her to walk into the school by herself because he thought she might just have a heart attack from nerves. As he sat on the garden seat George tried to master his own nerves.

Come on George, he chided himself, *pull yourself together*. But his heart still seemed to be doing a crazy dance in his chest with his stomach as a partner.

"Come on, Maggie, you can look at the flowers at lunch time; we're going to be late."

Maggie gave George a fleeting look of annoyance but joined his side again and they finished the walk to the front door of the school.

The reception area for the school was decorated richly. The walls were painted in beautiful shimmering gold and the two lounges to their right, in front of the service window, were covered in rich purple velvet and looked very inviting. The ground was covered in tiles with little pictures of ancient looking fairies and George wondered why on earth they had kept such a big, extravagant building for only fifteen children.

George led the way to the service window where a bothered looking old woman sat shuffling papers while muttering to herself.

"I have half a mind..."

"Excuse me," George said politely. "I'm George Mutton and this is my sister Maggie. Today is our first day of school and we're not sure where to go."

The old reception lady, who was wearing a name tag which read *Mildred*, stared at George with her sharp, beady eyes.

"You go to class, that's where you go."

George felt a slight flush cross his face.

"Well..." George started uncertainly, "do you know where our classes are?"

The old woman glared at him for a second and then heaved a great sigh and hoisted herself out of her chair. She shuffled out of sight and then reappeared next to the service window, made from a door that blended perfectly with the wall.

"Well come on," Mildred snapped, rolling her eyes. "I didn't just nearly break my back for your entertainment; follow me."

George and Maggie hurried over to the old woman and walked silently in her wake. They passed about a dozen empty classrooms before Mildred stopped outside of a somewhat occupied one. It had only five pupils in it.

"This will be the girl's classroom," Mildred said, snapping her eyes to Maggie.

Maggie started at being addressed as such and hurried into the room with a small, scared glance at George. He grabbed her hand and squeezed it, giving her what he hoped was a reassuring smile. Mildred started walking again and George followed silently. Every now and then Mildred would cluck her tongue irritably and look back at him.

"This is your classroom here, boy. You're bordering on late for your first day, did you know? I'd smarten up by tomorrow, if I were you."

And with that, Mildred started to slowly shuffle back the way she came.

George entered his new classroom with his heart pumping wildly. He was more nervous than he had ever been in his life and wondered briefly how he would feel if no one liked him. The door swung open and George saw five kids, around the same age as he was, turn their heads to look at him.

There were three boys and two girls. One of the girls wore her long black hair in pigtails and, even on first appearance, seemed snobby. The other girl, obviously that pigtailed girl's friend, had shocking red hair and gave an annoyingly high-pitched giggle when she saw George and immediately started talking in whispers to her friend. Two of the boys nodded at George and beckoned him over to them. The boys were both blond and tall. They were trying to get the girls' attention by throwing paper at them.

"Hi, I'm Matty," the taller one said, extending his hand.

George shook it, mumbling his own name in reply, suddenly very conscious of his spiky hair and short height.

"And I'm Billy."

George shook the other boy's hand too, and turned to introduce himself to the third boy in the room, who had black hair and very pale skin. Billy grabbed him and turned him back around.

"You don't wanna do that," he said, with a contemptuous look at the black-haired boy.

"Why?" George asked, looking again at the boy, trying to find something that could be bad about him.

"He's a freak," Matty said, with a laugh. "He's a loser. It'd be really stupid of you to talk to him; you'd become an instant loser too."

George looked at the two boys laughing cruelly, then looked again at the black-haired boy. George could see him blushing. He had obviously heard Matty and Billy's comments about him and George felt a huge pang of pity, but an even bigger wave of anger. He turned to the two blond boys.

"You know what? He looks like he at least has some brains, which is more than I could say about either of you."

And then George swiftly turned from the two stunned-looking boys and walked over to the other boy, to sit next to him.

The black-haired boy stared at George in shock for a few seconds. "What are you doing? Those boys will torture you if you sit near me; I'm like a disease."

George laughed. "Look, mate, I don't care how much they hate me. Must be better than having them as friends."

14

The black-haired boy let out a small laugh and extended his hand. "Charlie Redwin."

George shook his hand and told Charlie his name. George was just about to ask Charlie what their teacher was like when she walked into the classroom. George's new teacher had long, wavy blonde hair tied back in a ponytail, a nice smile and pleasant rosy cheeks.

"Wow! She's pretty," George whispered to Charlie.

"Yeah, and she's really nice, too."

"It seems that we have a new member of our class," the pretty teacher said smiling kindly at George. "George, I am Miss Roland. Perhaps you could stand up and introduce yourself to all of us. Give us a bit of information on yourself."

George swallowed thickly and stood up on shaky legs; he had not been expecting this.

"Ummm...hey," he mumbled lamely, feeling a hot red flush rise in his cheeks. "The name's George Mutton. I had to move here because my mum's about to have twins and...that's it."

George sat down hurriedly, completely aware that he sounded like an idiot. Matty and Billy sniggered, shaking their heads menacingly at George, while the girls let off another round of ear-piercing giggles.

"That's lovely, George," Miss Roland said, seemingly oblivious to the terrible embarrassment George was suffering. "And now for some math..."

xxx

George's second day had a much better feel about it, now that he at least had a friend to depend on. Charlie and George had struck up a friendship instantly. Charlie was a quiet boy who frequently stuttered and spoke with his eyes lowered to the floor, while George was the complete opposite; they seemed to be two halves to a whole and were both grateful for each other's company.

"Good morning, class," Miss Roland said in a sing-song voice as she swept into the classroom.

"Good Morning, Miss Roland," the class chanted back— except for the girl with the black hair.

The teacher stopped in front of the girl with a hurt look on her face.

"Miss Redwin? Don't you wish me a good morning?" Miss Roland stared at the girl with black hair as she glared up at her.

"Redwin?" George whispered to Charlie. "Are you related to her?"

Charlie looked at George incredulously.

"Of course I am; she's my twin sister Yvonne. Couldn't you see the resemblance? Wow, you really don't pay much attention, do you, mate?"

George looked back at Charlie's sister and now realized that, yes, she was a confident, snooty, female version of Charlie.

Miss Roland had walked away from Yvonne and sat down at her desk.

"If anyone does not reply to my 'good morning' from now on, they will be put into detention for being rude," she said, giving Yvonne a pointed look. "Is that quite understood?"

"Yes, Miss Roland," the class chanted back, including Yvonne.

"Now, class, please extract your copies of *The Mysterious Mount Dusk* from your bags and read chapter five in silence while I talk to Miss Redwin outside for a minute."

Yvonne huffily got out of her seat and stormed outside. Miss Roland followed her and closed the classroom door behind them. As if they were reading each other's minds, Charlie and George instantly jumped out of their seats and ran to the door, ears pressed eagerly at the large, old-fashioned key hole.

"That was quite unacceptable, Yvonne," they heard Miss Roland saying. "I will not be humiliated by my students in my classroom. If it happens again, I will call your Uncle Hubert."

The two boys heard Yvonne give a mean little giggle.

"Oh yes, Uncle Hubert. I do believe that your mother knew

my uncle, Miss Roland. Uncle Hubert was just telling me last night of our family's connection to yours."

There was silence for a few moments and then they heard Miss Roland reply with her voice shaking.

"Yvonne, I am well aware of both our families' history but the...conflict happened a long time ago, before you or I were even born, and I expect you to leave your personal opinions of me and my family out of my classroom, do you understand? Does Charlie know about your family history?"

Yvonne laughed again.

"That little do-gooder? Ha! Uncle Hubert tried to get Charlie involved but he lacks certain noble family traits that are essential to hearing the full story."

George felt Charlie tense up next to him.

"He does not even care that our parents perished to uphold the family name. No, Charlie has not heard what I was told last night. Don't worry, Miss, he still respects you."

Charlie and George looked at each other. It was obvious to George from the look on Charlie's face that he too was very confused, without a clue about what his twin sister had apparently heard the night before.

"Miss Redwin, you will behave from now on. It is...very sad to me...that you have taken this attitude, and I can see that I will not be able to make you understand the other side of the story. I simply ask that you treat me with at least a bit of respect at school. Now, sit down and read with the rest of your class."

Charlie and George scrambled back to their seats just in time. Yvonne stalked back to her chair, sat down and violently flicked the pages of her book until she found the right one. Miss Roland quietly sat down at her desk, her face tense and sad.

"You have to find out what your sister knows. Sounds like it'd be something interesting," George whispered to his new friend.

"I'll try," Charlie whispered back uncertainly. "But I know how good my family is at keeping secrets."

CHAPTER 3

Redwin and Regale

George spent the next two days getting to know his new friend. It was a pleasant surprise for George to discover that Charlie knew a lot of interesting facts about Mount Dusk, such as the rumor that the peak of Mount Dusk was supposed to be haunted so nobody living in Mount Dusk ever went there. Then the fact that, hundreds of years before, the town had been abandoned and was re-opened only ninety years ago. Before it was re-opened, the town of Mount Dusk had been known as Regale Point, named after a rich family who started the town. The two boys were sitting under a big, shady tree at the front of Mount Dusk Academy. School had just finished and George was listening to Charlie explain what he knew about the abandonment of Mount Dusk.

"I heard from my old Aunt Martha that there were two really famous families who lived in the town. One family owned a local circus and magic show and the other had built the school and had heaps of money. Then all of a sudden, bam! Both families disappeared and no one ever heard of them again—cool, huh?"

George stared above him at the cloudy purple-grey sky, trying to figure out how so many people could just disappear.

"Yeah, that is pretty cool...you know I swear I've seen the name *Regale* somewhere," George said slowly, wracking his brain to try and remember where he'd heard the old name before.

"It was probably just in a school book. I think they mention it in that book we read for history *The Mysterious Mount Dusk*."

George and Charlie chatted for a while about the two mysterious families and where they could be now and then set off for home.

"Where do you live?" George asked Charlie

Charlie grimaced.

"With my uncle on Willow Street."

"Where all the big castles are?" George asked incredulously.

The previous day George's dad had picked him up from school and taken him to have a look at the massive dwellings on Willow Street.

"Yeah that's the one," Charlie muttered un-enthusiastically.

"I'd love to live there!" George exclaimed. "Can I come see your house?"

Charlie's face reddened and he avoided looking at George. "My Uncle...well...he's not very nice; there's no other way to say it," Charlie said this in a rush, reddening more than George thought possible.

"Do you mean he's old and cranky? Because I don't mind old and cranky; my grandpa takes the cake when it comes to that. Last time I saw him he told me that I wasn't growing at a healthy rate and if my mum didn't start to feed me more meat I'd be a girl by the time I was fifteen...I don't think mum ever invited him around again after that."

Charlie stopped walking; they had arrived at the top of Willow Street.

"Look..." Charlie started uncomfortably, "he isn't just old and cranky. It's hard to explain. But I'll see you tomorrow; it's Saturday, so I can show you the peak of Mount Dusk, if you want."

George agreed to see the top of Mount Dusk; he was extremely curious to discover if it actually was haunted or not. He said goodbye to Charlie, turned and started to walk the rest of the way to his house. George grinned to himself; it seemed that he had found what he'd always hoped for; a mystery and a famous one at that. George decided then and there that he would look into the disappearances of the two old families. After all, it couldn't hurt.

xxx

The next morning George met Charlie in front of George's house to go and explore Mount Dusk. They were about to leave when they heard a loud, violent cough behind them. George turned around and saw Maggie standing there, hands on hips, her face a dangerous shade of red.

"I want to come," she said in a deadly soft voice.

"No, Maggie, go and find your own friends," George said impatiently.

He had to endure his sister's constant nagging while living with her; he didn't need it when he was trying to hang out with his friends.

"MUM!" Maggie suddenly screamed making the two boys jump with shock. "GEORGE WONT LET ME WALK WITH HIM!"

Mrs. Mutton appeared at the door of the house looking agitated. "George, dear, just let her go with you. What harm can she do? Now go on and enjoy your day."

George felt anger burn through him as he looked into his little sister's smug face. "Why do you even want to hang out with people who don't want you around?" George hissed at her, grabbing her arm to hurry her up.

"Because," she said loftily, "the other option is to stay in the house, listen to Dad run into things and Mum talk about nothing but babies. Yech!"

George had to admit that Maggie had a point there. Mrs. Mutton's new favorite activity was to shove tiny, knitted things under your nose, squealing, "Oh how lovely is it?" while you tried to edge your way out of the room to freedom.

"Fine," George said, resigning himself to the worst. "But we're not stopping for you if you get tired. It's a long walk and, if you're going to come, you have to keep up."

Maggie smiled and walked on ahead of them, touching flowers on the side of the path and humming in a high-pitched tone.

"She's not so bad," Charlie said after a while. "At least she seems to like you."

George started to feel uncomfortable; he felt that he should say, "I'm sure your sister likes you too," but he was not so sure that she did. George was very curious to learn more about Charlie's family but Charlie seemed to get uncomfortable talking about them.

They walked for about an hour, chatting idly about school and George's new house, when suddenly Maggie stopped dead in her tracks about ten meters in front of them and let out a small, strangled scream. The two boys rushed forward, looking in Maggie's direction, but all George could see was a tree.

"What's wrong?" George asked his sister, still looking around wildly.

"That...that tree, it just...had a...a face!"

George and Charlie looked at each other then started to laugh.

"Maggie, the bark probably just looked like a face. Trees don't have faces."

The boys kept on laughing as Maggie's face turned dangerously red again.

"Look, I'm telling you it wasn't just the bark! It was a face...it looked like it was smiling. I want to go home!"

George was laughing harder than ever. *A tree with a face— a face that was smiling?*

"I WANT MY MUM!" Maggie suddenly cried, tears welling up in her terrified eyes.

George stopped laughing abruptly. He could not believe that his sister was so upset about such a crazy idea.

"Maggie, it's just not possible, so don't be scared. You can't be scared of something that's impossible."

But no amount of logic would convince Maggie that it had not been real, so they headed back home. George looked at his sister as they were walking. Maggie was a pain, but she normally lacked the imagination that George had. Maggie never made up stories unless she was annoyed and wanted her own way about something. Maggie was hugging herself, her head was down and she was staring somberly at her feet.

George put an arm around her and she rested her head on his arm for the rest of the journey home. It was only lunch time when they arrived back and Maggie wasted no time in telling Mrs. Mutton that George had walked her into a haunted forest then laughed at her when she cried.

Mrs. Mutton told George off and reminded him that Maggie was only seven and that the "poor thing" wasn't adjusting well to the new town. After the lecture from his mother George stormed out of the house to where Charlie was waiting for him at his driveway gates.

"She…is…unbelievable!" George exploded.

Charlie laughed and they started walking without a destination in mind.

"You know," Charlie said, "Maggie isn't the only one who's seen something on the top of the mountain."

George laughed. "Yeah but, a face on a tree? That's ridiculous; she just wanted to be a pain…"

But George was a bit suspicious; he remembered how scared she had looked.

"Well, I think there's something weird going on at the top of Mount Dusk, even if Maggie didn't see that face," Charlie said confidently.

"Yeah, maybe," George answered, lost in his own thoughts.

XXX

It was dinner time at the Mutton residence. The family was eating a delicious meal of roast chicken with potatoes and everyone was recapping their first week of school and work.

"Well, my teacher is horrible," Maggie whined loudly. "He just talks and talks. He never asks questions and we do nothing except write notes."

"At least you're learning; never take that for granted, Maggie," Mrs. Mutton said sternly across the table. "George dear, please shut the curtains. It's getting dark."

George swallowed his mouthful and walked over to the curtains. And then he saw it—*Thomas Regale* embroidered on his lounge room curtains. That's where he had heard the name Regale! It was in his house all along!

George ran from the room, his family staring curiously after him. He reached the phone in the hallway and dialed Charlie's number. Charlie had only very reluctantly given George his home number just in case his uncle answered. The phone rang.

"Hello?" A haughty female voice answered the phone.

"Oh, hello, Yvonne. Is Charlie there?" George heard Yvonne drop the phone.

"Charlie! Phone!"

"Hello?" This time it was Charlie.

"You'll never guess what I found. Can you come over? You can sleep here. I think we're going to have a lot to talk about..."

Charlie arrived half an hour later and Mrs. Mutton made him some dinner from the left-over chicken.

"Thank you," Charlie muttered shyly and took the sandwiches into George's room.

"I found out where I saw the name *Regale*...my curtains!" George exploded as soon as the bedroom door shut. "I think they must have lived in this house before they disappeared!"

Charlie was chewing a mouthful of chicken sandwich, his brow furrowed.

"Well...even if that was true, why do I care again? I mean, that's cool and all, but why are you so excited?"

George looked at Charlie incredulously. How could this not be exciting news? The people involved in the biggest mystery of the town had lived here, in George's house, and even though George wasn't sure how, he knew that he was one step closer to discovering what had happened hundreds of years ago when the Regale family went missing.

"Charlie, we have to figure out what happened to the Regales. A whole community can't just disappear without a trace!"

Charlie laughed, choking a little on his sandwich.

"George, how are we going to solve a mystery that big? No one, in hundreds of years, has ever figured out what happened to the Regales or that circus family. Nobody even knows what the circus family's name was; there are no records of them anywhere."

"Maybe no one cared to look closely enough. All I know is that I can't just hear about this mystery and leave it. We have to at least try. Come on, Charlie, it'll be fun! We'll be like two awesome detectives."

Charlie stared at George for a few seconds then sighed.

"Okay, George we'll look into it, but I'm warning you— don't get your hopes up about solving anything. This town is as good at keeping secrets as my family, I reckon."

Now it was George's turn to stare at Charlie for a few seconds. Charlie's family. For some reason the mystery of Charlie's family intrigued him almost as much the mystery of the Regales. Then George remembered the overheard conversation between Yvonne and Miss Roland.

"Hey, did you ever find out what your sister was talking to Miss Roland about?" George asked enthusiastically.

"Nah," Charlie answered gloomily. "When I asked my uncle to tell me he told me that, even though I was a Redwin, the Redwin story would be wasted on me. Probably just some stupid family honor story...like I care, anyway."

George could hear the bitterness in Charlie's voice and felt sorry for him. It must be hard to be an outcast in your own family. George really wanted to ask about Charlie's parents and what had happened to them but he didn't want to upset Charlie. He remembered Yvonne saying something about them dying for their family's honor.

"Hey, Charlie, has your family always been rich? They sound pretty snooty, always talking about family honor and everything."

"Yeah, I think so," Charlie replied thoughtfully. "I've always lived in large houses, we've always had a maid too—she's the friendliest person in my whole house. There are family coats of arms everywhere, so either my Uncle's just a nutter, or, yeah, I'm from one of those rich families, I guess. Never really thought about it myself."

Charlie paused, looking forlorn.

"I wish I could have a family like yours. You don't have a maid, but people smile at you and hope you're well. Your mum makes you breakfast in the morning and your dad tells those old man jokes. My Uncle is as mean as they come and I'm telling you now, George, you do not want to meet him."

George spent the rest of the evening trying to convince Charlie to let him stay over at his house and after four hours of whispered argument, (George's mum would've had a fit if she knew how late they had stayed awake), Charlie agreed that the following weekend he could stay. George grinned at his success but, when he looked over at Charlie and saw how worried he looked, the grin was wiped from his face. George contented his uneasy conscience by telling himself that after next weekend Charlie would know that no matter how awful his uncle was, George would always be his friend.

xxx

The next week at school was very challenging for George. Because he had arrived at Mount Dusk Academy halfway through term, he had a lot of catching up to do and his attempts to ignore the two thick-headed class bullies, Matty and Billy, were equally as hard. George constantly fought a silent internal battle with himself, trying not to smack one of them in the back of the head.

On Tuesday morning George sat down behind Billy and, staring at the big blond head, he made a hasty decision. George ripped a page out of his school exercise book and wrote a quick message on it: *I can't sleep without my pink teddy*. He then pulled out his mini roll of sticky tape and lined the top of the page with it.

"Hey, Billy," George called, suppressing a laugh.

"Huh? What?" Billy replied, slowly narrowing his piggy eyes.

"I just want to congratulate you, mate. You really know how to talk to the girls."

With a quick movement, George slapped Billy on his broad back in mock congratulations, subtly sticking the message there.

"Yeah, bet you wish you had my kinda skills," Billy said stupidly, laughing to himself.

George joined in the laughter and Billy, looking confused and worried about George's mental state, turned back around.

Charlie joined George a few minutes later and, when he spotted the note on Billy's back, he burst into hysterical laughter.

"What you laughing at, freak?" Billy asked glaring at Charlie.

"Oh, just our inferior knowledge of females," George reassured him with false seriousness on his face.

Charlie gave George a high five under the desk, still smiling broadly, a twinkle of success in his eyes.

The rest of the week was spent paying for this little prank as Matty and Billy tripped, Chinese-burned and glared menacingly at George and Charlie at every given opportunity. But after three days of this treatment, it was Friday afternoon and school was almost over. George was excited. He had his clothes for the next day in his school bag so that he could go straight over to Charlie's house after school without the need to go home first.

Charlie had been a little bit quiet all day and George knew that he was nervous about George meeting his uncle.

The bell rang for the end of school and George jumped up out of his seat, narrowly missed Billy's outstretched foot, and headed straight for the door. Charlie got up reluctantly, following his friend out of the school grounds. On the way to Charlie's, George tried to imagine what Charlie's uncle looked like. He imagined a tall, dark and sinister-looking man, stalking about his big house barking demands at everyone. George wasn't at all nervous about meeting Charlie's uncle. Even if he was mean to George, it seemed like he was just mean to everyone, so it really wouldn't be anything personal, anyway.

The two boys reached the top of Willow Street and stopped. Charlie looked over at George. "Last chance to back out..."

George grinned. "No way, I've been looking forward to this all week!"

Charlie sighed and shook his head, but a little smile was on his lips as he did so. There was just no stopping George when he was curious.

On the way down to Charlie's house at the other end of the street they passed huge manors with expensive looking cars inside the tall gates that guarded against curious passers-by. George stared and *wow*-ed at every one and Charlie let out a reluctant laugh at his friend's behavior.

Then George saw it. The biggest house on the street. Well it wasn't really a house; it was a castle. A castle with turrets and a beautiful sloping lawn leading to the massive front doors.

"This is your house? You live in this?" George asked, absolutely astounded.

Charlie laughed. "Well it may be big but it's really cold; it's too big to heat properly...I'm always freezing."

George kept on staring with his mouth open.

"Who cares about cold? This is the best house I've ever seen!"

Charlie laughed again, looked slightly happier and led the way to the front door. Charlie knocked on the massive redwood door using a metal knocker that was in the shape of an old-fashioned bicycle wheel. After a few seconds George heard a number of locks click and the door opened to reveal an old lady with neatly cut, short grey hair and a perfectly pressed white apron over her plain black dress.

"Why, hello, master Charlie, and who is your friend?"

Charlie smiled warmly at the old woman.

"Rosemary, this is George; he will be staying over tonight."

Rosemary looked delighted and George realized that Charlie probably would never have brought a friend home before.

"Well that's lovely, dear. I'll make sure I cook an extra tasty dinner for you both."

Rosemary took their school bags and tottered off, her footsteps echoing in the cavernous entrance. After hearing about how awful Charlie's family could be, George was glad that there was a friendly woman to act as a mother in this large, cold home. Charlie's house was built along the same lines as Mount Dusk Academy. The ceilings were very high, and elaborate stained glass windows cast colors over everything—deep reds, rich purples and glittering golds.

Charlie stood there looking uncomfortable and then gestured for George to follow him. Charlie led him to a lovely staircase with highly polished gold banisters. As they walked up the stairs their footfalls echoed loudly off the far ceiling. When they reached the landing George was surprised again; he had never seen so many doors in the one house before. He estimated that there must have been about twenty doors. Charlie quickly crossed the landing and entered the room directly in front of them. George stepped into Charlie's room and gasped. Charlie's bed was about as big as George's whole room, with gold hangings above it. The floor was covered in a thick, expensive-looking rug and, best of all, he had a television the size of a small cinema screen on the wall facing his bed.

George looked at Charlie with his mouth hanging open. Charlie laughed and looked a bit more at ease.

"Well...this is it." Charlie said, crossing the room to sit on his bed.

"Charlie, how could you have kept this from me?" George asked, laughing. "I can't believe it! You're so lucky!"

Charlie's smile faltered a little. "Yeah I guess..." he muttered.

"I have to see the rest of this house!"

Charlie led George around the castle showing him furniture made hundreds of years ago, art pieces of strange disfigured bodies and elaborately dressed men and woman in golden jeweled masks that were hung everywhere around the house and carpets so thick and soft that you sunk a few centimeters when you stood on one. When they reached the narrow staircase that led to the towers, Charlie paused.

"It's kind of spooky up there."

George scoffed. "All the more reason to carry on."

After the climb to the tower the boys entered a dusty brick room with a view that took George's breath away. George looked out of the window which was arched and had no glass in it so that an icy wind ripped through the room, adding to the chilled blue atmosphere that hung empty and cold.

As far as the eye could see there were fields and forest; it was very beautiful indeed. George wandered around the room; it was littered with broken bits of furniture and old ragged books. Charlie had been right. It was a bit spooky and George was just about to turn and leave when a movement caught his eye. Yvonne was crouched behind a broken bookshelf, hiding, with a little diary hugged close to her chest.

"Oh!" Charlie exclaimed when he spotted her.

"Get out! I'm trying to write, you little idiot!" Yvonne screeched at Charlie, and looked thoroughly embarrassed.

"You keep a diary, Yvonne? You mean you have feelings?" Charlie asked with suppressed laughter, making his voice tight.

"OUT!" Yvonne started throwing bits of debris at her twin brother.

The two boys laughed all the way back to Charlie's bedroom.

"So she *is* human. I was starting to wonder," George chuckled.

Soon after, Rosemary served a wonderful dinner of steak, mashed potatoes and roast vegetables that the boys ate in Charlie's room. Charlie was relaxed and smiling until they heard the front doors open and close.

"Uncle Hubert," Charlie said quietly, looking suddenly nervous.

George heard somebody walking up the staircase—then a pause. George and Charlie looked at each other. The door swung open to reveal a man in his mid-fifties with a rounded belly and small cold eyes. His nose pointed straight up and a look of superiority flared his large hairy nostrils.

"Charlie, I was not informed of our visitor for this evening," Uncle Hubert said in a slow, deadly voice, without looking at George.

Charlie looked nervously into his uncle's face. "Sorry, Uncle Hubert...I couldn't find you last night to ask you."

Uncle Hubert stared at Charlie for a moment then turned to George.

"Well...good evening to you. I am Charlie's uncle; you may call me Mister Redwin."

"Nice to meet you, Mister Redwin," George replied quietly, afraid that he had gotten Charlie into trouble.

"You boys are not to disturb me tonight. I will be in the study...sorting out a few affairs, then I will be out until late. You are both to be in bed by the time I return. Is that quite understood?"

George and Charlie nodded and Uncle Hubert swept from the room.

George looked at Charlie, whose face was red; he looked thoroughly embarrassed.

"Sorry..." he mumbled, turning away.

George put a smile back on his face and walked over to Charlie's bed.

"Ha, forget about him. What do you want to watch? Got any good movies?"

XXX

At nearly midnight they heard Uncle Hubert leave.

"What was he doing in the study for so long?" George asked.

"I don't know," Charlie said, turning off the television. They had just been watching a horror movie that had been quite satisfactorily frightening.

"He's always in the study 'sorting out a few affairs'; I've never really known what he does in there."

George turned to grin wickedly at Charlie, "Well, then, the time has come to finally solve that mystery."

And with that, George bounded off the bed, across the room and out onto the landing before Charlie could object. He was feeling rather reckless, having just watched a movie involving spies.

"No!" Charlie whispered urgently, catching up to George. "Yvonne is about somewhere; she'll go straight to Uncle Hubert if she finds us."

"Well, then, you better stop talking or she'll hear us," George whispered back as he crept along the long hallway.

After a dozen or so doors George saw a plaque on a door which read: **Keep Out, Private**.

"Guessing this is it?" George whispered to Charlie.

Charlie nodded and looked around nervously for any sign of his sister. George opened the door slowly, praying that it wouldn't creak. The room inside was round like George's room. The Redwin family coat of arms sat impressively on the wall opposite the door and a handsome fireplace cast flickering shadows across the room.

Once George and Charlie were safely inside, George shut the door again as Charlie crept over to the only desk in the room and started opening drawers. George tiptoed over to an enormous pile of folders and started looking through them. It seemed that the folders were just full of records of some sort.

"Hold on!" George said, realization washing over him. "These are records of all the inhabitants that Mount Dusk has ever had...what would your uncle want with these?"

Charlie walked over from the desk and snatched another folder up. "Wow, these records are from the sixteenth century!"

George and Charlie quickly flipped through the folders, every now and then letting out exclamations of surprise at how old the records were. George's mind was reeling. What was Charlie's uncle doing with all these records every night?

Charlie suddenly grabbed George's arm. "George, Uncle Hubert has all the records of the Regale family! Its looks like the family disappeared in...1795."

George hurried to read over Charlie's shoulder. He scanned the page for 1795: Thomas Regale, Lillian Regale, Annabelle Regale, Francis Regale, Maria Regale, Gwyneth Regale. Then George looked at the page for 1796...no Regales were mentioned.

"So...whatever happened to the Regales happened before the New Year of 1796 since all of the lists are dated as written on New Year's Day of every year."

George furrowed his brow in concentration...what did this mean? George looked over at Charlie, who was staring at the lists, eyes wide.

"I think I know why my uncle has these records," Charlie said quietly, turning to George.

"There were two families who disappeared at the same time...the Regales and the Redwins. Remember I told you about that circus family who disappeared at the same time as the Regales?"

George snatched the record out of Charlie's hand. The list for 1795 ended with five Redwins: Millicent Redwin, Phillip Redwin, Jackson Redwin, Catherine Redwin, Christopher Redwin.

George and Charlie looked at each other hardly believing their eyes.

"Your ancestor's were...that circus family who disappeared at the same time as the Regales?"

Charlie looked thoughtful. "Maybe...who knows? Might just be a coincidence."

George suddenly jumped up and started rummaging through more papers.

"What are you looking for?" Charlie asked

"Your family tree; your uncle's obsessed with your family. He has to have one and if we can match the dates and names of the Redwins in the records to the Redwins on your family tree then that'll prove it—you're a descendant of the Redwins on that list...and the circus family."

Charlie started sifting through papers too, and in a couple of minutes gave a yell of triumph.

"Found it!"

George ran over and the two boys scanned the giant piece of ancient-looking parchment held in Charlie's trembling hand.

"Here!" George yelled. "Millicent, Phillip, Jackson, Catherine and Christopher Redwin! And the dates match!"

Charlie looked astounded. "So it was my family who disappeared? Wow, I wonder what happened to them. And why no one has found out that at least one Redwin survived whatever happened. They could have questioned them and asked them personally what happened."

"Well, remember what you said about all of the records disappearing with the families that first day you told me about the Regales? So nobody would have known what family to look for with all the records gone." George reminded Charlie. "Looks like your family not only disappeared but they took the town records with them. What a suspicious thing to do."

George was just about to start rummaging for more hidden treasure when he heard a sound that turned his blood cold—the front door opening with a sickening creak. George and Charlie gave each other a fleeting look of terror then ran as fast as they could out the door. George hastily closed the door behind them and the two boys raced to Charlie's room just in time to hear someone start climbing the stairs. Both boys slumped onto Charlie's bed in relief, then Charlie suddenly sat bolt upright again, his face drained of color, eyes wide with horror.

"We didn't put the family tree back in its right spot! If Uncle Hubert sees it, he'll know someone's been in his study!"

The two boys sat in silence, straining their ears to hear where Uncle Hubert would go—to the study or to bed? If he went straight to bed then one of the boys could sneak back into the study and put everything right. If he went to the study...

"*Aaargh!*" A distant cry of rage.

"Pretend to be asleep!" Charlie whispered urgently. The two boys scrambled into Charlie's massive bed and, hearts pumping wildly, tried to even out their breathing. They heard Charlie's bedroom door open and Uncle Hubert's shoes clunk across the hard wood floor. George didn't even dare to breathe. He kept his eyes determinedly closed and tried to make his face look relaxed and deeply asleep. After a couple of minutes, in which George suspected Uncle Hubert was watching for any sign of liveliness, they heard Uncle Hubert clunk back to the door, pause, then quietly shut the door behind him. Both boys let out their breath and turned to face each other under the safety of Charlie's blankets.

"I wonder who he'll think went in..." Charlie started then they heard Uncle Hubert's voice booming up the stairs.

"Rosemary! How many times have I asked you not to clean in my study?"

"Oh no!" Charlie moaned, "Don't blame Rosemary!"

They heard Rosemary splutter, completely nonplussed.

"If it was not you, Rosemary, then you had better know who it was, considering that it was you in charge of looking after the children in my absence, and that includes enforcing boundaries!"

The two boys were surprised to hear Rosemary say, "So sorry, Mister Redwin, it will not happen again. I am afraid that it was me who entered your study, a lapse in sensible thinking."

Rosemary said the last few words a little louder. George suspected that she wanted the boys to hear her disapproval of breaking the rules, but certainly did not want them to endure Uncle Hubert's displeasure. George looked at Charlie, his small, pale face screwed up with guilt.

"I didn't want Rosemary to get blamed; I swear I'll never go in that study again."

George was bursting to say, "Don't be stupid we have to go in there again!" but thought that this might not be the time to say it with Charlie feeling so awfully guilty about Rosemary being blamed for their crime. George rolled over onto his side and closed his eyes; his mind was reeling. He was sleeping next to one of the most recent descendants of the famous Mount Dusk circus family. Could the mystery of Redwin and Regale possibly get more interesting than this?

CHAPTER 4

Garden of Souls

George spent the rest of the week trying to drop subtle hints (that were none too subtle) that Charlie should re-enter his uncle's study.

"Charlie do you reckon Yvonne's been allowed in the study? Isn't it unfair that you don't get to?" or "I'd say it's your duty to know about your own family history, I mean, it is your family."

But Charlie would just give George an exasperated look and shake his head. George was burning to learn about Charlie's family history. After all, they had been involved in Mount Dusk's biggest scandal, but it was not as much fun to do it alone. He wanted Charlie to help him solve this mystery and he decided to exhaust all his efforts of persuasion on his reluctant friend. After three days of his friend's nagging, Charlie still wouldn't go inside his uncle's study again, but agreed to accompany George on a late night expedition to the peak of Mount Dusk. George's plan was to re-kindle Charlie's sense of adventure with this trip to the supposedly haunted destination. George was excited for the rest of the week thinking about it. Sometimes he considered cancelling it and just having a quiet weekend where he wasn't defying his parents but the irresistible pull of mystery stifled any prolonged caution.

So, late on Friday night the two boys sneaked out of their houses armed with a torch each and a flask of hot chocolate provided by George. George had never misbehaved like this before in his life, sneaking out of home, but something about the town of Mount Dusk made George feel reckless. It may have been the wild wilderness that surrounded him with every step he took through the town, or just the mystery that seemed to lurk around every corner. It hadn't been easy sneaking out. With every loud snore from Mr. Mutton, George had jumped a mile and scampered back to his room with his heart beating frantically.

The two friends met at George's back fence with a grave nod to each other and silently crept up the winding path leading to the peak of Mount Dusk, both contemplating what would happen to them if they were caught. George swallowed loudly as he thought of the look of fury that would cloud his mother's face, the look of disappointment that would make his father's expression sag with worry, or the infuriating smugness of Maggie when he was punished.

The sounds of night surrounded them as they cautiously walked the mountain path. Owls hooted, leaves crinkled in the breeze and the crushing silence of night pressed heavily on their ears. Cold winds nipped at their faces and summoned goose bumps up their arms. As they reached the peak they began searching around them for a good place to settle. George's stomach felt as if it was doing back flips. He would be lying if he had said that he wasn't scared but with his fear came the determination that spurred him on; he just had to get Charlie involved in something exciting so that he would be more agreeable to investigating Uncle Hubert. Charlie looked small and nervous as he stood in front of George shivering with his gloved fingers in his mouth. George could see that his friend was shaking all over and his eyes were wide and apprehensive, swiveling around in his head in search of lurking danger.

George broke the silence. "Come on, let's sit down and have a drink."

The two boys cleared an area of sticks and leaves so that they could sit down, their progress hampered by thick gloves making them clumsy. George managed to get most of the hot chocolate into cups and the boys sat drinking, slowly letting the warm drink relax them. A sweet feeling of comfort settled in George and he smiled for the first time that night.

"I wonder if we'll see anything worthwhile," Charlie said, looking a bit better with color in his cheeks from the hot drink.

"It doesn't matter if we don't," George said. "This is pretty cool and creepy without ghosts...hope Mum hasn't noticed that I'm gone."

George got a sick feeling in his stomach at this last thought so he tried to push it from his mind.

"Yeah," Charlie said, nodding emphatically, "If Uncle Hubert ever found out I'd be dead for cert..." But Charlie was cut off by a distant sound. A long moan carried on the wind making both boys freeze with wide, scared eyes.

"Was that the wind?" Charlie asked, sounding hopeful.

"If it was," George said slowly "then the wind has suddenly got vocal cords."

The boys sat in silence for a few minutes straining their ears for any other unnatural sounds. George suddenly became aware that this had been a very bad idea; they were out here all alone, no one knew where they were and they had no means to defend themselves. He started looking around for something to use as a weapon but he doubted very much that anything would work against a ghost...and then it happened. Over the roaring wind they heard a shriek, a high-pitched shriek of pain that reverberated up the boys' spines, leaving them stricken with horror.

"*Aaaaarrrgh!*" Both boys cried and started running in opposite directions.

Both had thrown their hot chocolate aside in panic. George had started running down the path back to town, thinking that the sound had come from the thick trees on the peak. He was halfway down the path when he realized that Charlie wasn't with him. Panic seared through his chest as he stood undecided on the path. Should he go home for help? Or go back up to the peak? In a flash he was racing back up the path, tears of fear running down his face, icy cold from the wind pelting him. He reached the spot where they had been drinking hot chocolate and spun around desperately trying to figure out which way Charlie had run.

"Oh no, no, no," George chanted, hoping against all hope that Charlie was alright.

He spotted a cup discarded over to his left and ran blindly in that direction, stumbling over sticks and low shrubs that scratched and snagged his clothing as he called breathlessly for his friend. He did this for the longest minute in his life until he saw Charlie ten feet in front of him, curled into a ball and sobbing in terror.

"Charlie!" George gasped and hurried to his friend's side.

"George, oh thank goodness!" Charlie replied, grabbing his friend tightly.

The two boys sat hugging each other for a few minutes until their hearts slowed down enough to allow speech and adequate embarrassment that they were, indeed, hugging.

"Why didn't you start running to town with me?" George asked in a whisper, too afraid to raise his voice in case something horrible was listening.

"I thought the noise was coming from the path," Charlie answered, shivering violently "I panicked."

George thought this was very odd because the sound to him had definitely come from the trees.

George looked cautiously around them. The trees cast

ghostly shadows in the dark, the wind making them move in a slow, demented dance.

"Let's get out of here, George," Charlie said, looking up at his friend.

"Yeah, good idea," George replied, standing up on weak legs that felt as if they were made of jelly.

The boys retraced their steps carefully, scared of straying deeper into the trees. They walked for a couple of minutes when Charlie suddenly stopped, a small squeak of surprise escaping him. George spun around and gasped. A tree directly behind them was watching them. Watching them. With gnarled eyes of bark. Charlie screamed, backed away too quickly and toppled over a tree root. George was frozen, staring at the tree face. *This cannot be happening*, George thought. It was a man's face, with thick eyebrows and a moustache; he opened his bark lips and let out a monstrous moan.

"*Heeeelp!*"

Charlie hid his face in the ground, sobbing uncontrollably, but George, filled with sudden bravery (or shock) spoke to the fearsome tree.

"Do...do you need help?" He asked lamely in a small, strangled voice.

The tree face stared at George then let out another moan on the breeze.

"*Yeeeeeees.*"

George swallowed, his mouth had suddenly gone very dry.

"Why?" He asked, not knowing why he was asking this and not running away at top speed. Perhaps it was the temporary uselessness of his weak legs.

The bark lips opened once more. "Me, my family, we are trapped here, in this wretched garden."

The tree face spoke as if the wind was his breath. It probably was, George suddenly realized.

"Why?" George asked again forgetting his fear a little bit and letting curiosity wash over him. "Who are you?"

A girl's voice suddenly spoke from behind them. "Redwin."

George and Charlie spun around and saw a female face protruding from another tree, her pretty visage made of bark.

"We are here because of Redwin; we are the Regales."

George's mind was spinning; nothing was making sense.

"But...but this is impossible! Can you get out? What do you mean you are here because of Redwin?"

The man's carved eyes looked intently at George.

"We are trapped. You must help us! Redwin is still among us, I can feel it!"

Charlie gave a fleeting look of horror to George, then got up and ran as fast as he could out of the trees.

George turned and whispered, "I'll be back," to the remarkable trees then followed Charlie as quickly as he could.

George caught up to Charlie on the path back to town. Charlie's face was red and swollen from crying.

"What *was* that?" Charlie screamed hysterically, "What on earth *was* that?"

George shook his head "I don't know exactly what that was...but I bet your uncle does. Charlie, we have to help those people, or those trees, or whatever they are and to do that I have a feeling that we're going to have to go back into that study and figure out what your ancestors were up to the year 1795."

Charlie looked daggers at George, "After all of that? The tree knew I was a Redwin, I'm sure of it, and you still want to go into that stupid study again?! I will never, ever go back in there, I will also never go up this path again, do you understand? Just drop it, George! Before you get us both killed! Haunted trees, disappearances, it's too much! Do you understand me, George? This has gone too far! Talking to trees in the middle of the night is where I'm drawing the line."

And with that Charlie ran off for his house, leaving George standing on the path feeling ashamed of himself. Charlie was terrified and all he could think about was his adventure of discovery. George sighed and made his way home, jumping at every shadow that moved. Tomorrow he would make it up to Charlie. The Regales were trapped in trees. *How awful*, George thought, as he turned and looked back up the mountain. A shiver slid down George's spine as he carried on home. He crept back into his house, and, luckily, no one seemed to have noticed his absence. Then gratefully he got into bed, mind buzzing. As he drifted into a weary sleep he thought he saw the leaf shape with *Thomas Regale* written in it glow slightly green, but sleep pulled George away from his room and into dreams of a forest of men all screaming for their souls.

CHAPTER 5

Detective Trio

*T*he next day, George started to walk up to Charlie's house, intent upon apologizing to his friend for being so insensitive. But as George rounded the corner where Willow Street was he bumped into a familiar face.

"Oh hey," Charlie said, laughing as he pulled himself up from the ground.

"Hey, I was just coming to see you," George said. "Look Charlie, I'm really sorry about last night; I was being an idiot."

Charlie smiled at his friend. "No, you were just being you, but thanks for apologizing. I brought a peace offering with me."

It was then that George noticed his friend's jumper bulging out the front in an odd rectangular shape.

"But we have to go somewhere secluded. No one can see this."

George grinned and led the way to his house, relieved that he and Charlie were on good terms again. They got inside, passed the stained windows and hastily went into George's room, locking the door behind them. With a flourish, Charlie pulled out a thick stack of different sized papers from his jumper, smiling triumphantly.

"Fresh from the study of Uncle Hubert," he proclaimed proudly.

George widened his eyes in shock. "You went back in there? Wow!"

The two boys jumped on George's bed, ready to sift through the forbidden paperwork when a shrill voice sounded from outside the bedroom door.

"George! I'm bored, let me in."

It was Maggie.

"Go away, Maggie!" George yelled, annoyed at his sister's bad timing.

"MUM!" Maggie screamed.

The boys hastily hid the papers under George's bed and George went to open the door. Maggie was standing there with a smug look on her face, a look that said, "Mum's going to make you play with me."

But they were all surprised when Mrs. Mutton shouted back, "Maggie, leave the boys alone!"

They all stood there looking at each other, confused. Mrs. Mutton bustled up the hallway, red in the face from the effort of walking around heavily pregnant.

"I'm sick of chasing you two around, so, new rule. If one of you has a friend over, then the other must learn to entertain themselves!"

George grinned in thanks to his mother while Maggie glared at her, mouth open.

"But, Mum..." George and Charlie heard Maggie start as she followed her mother up the hall.

"Geez, what's gotten into Mum?" George asked in wonder.

"Well, from the sounds of it, she's as sick of Maggie's whining as we are."

The boys laughed a bit until they heard the sound of soft

sobbing coming from Maggie's room next door. George stood still wondering whether to ignore Maggie and just carry on but the sound of the crying put him off and with a sigh he set off for Maggie's room.

"Maggie?" George called gently, opening the door.

Maggie was sitting on her bed staring out of the window crying softly.

"Maggie, me and Charlie have important...things to do. It's really secret, otherwise I'd let you play with us."

Maggie looked over at George. "But why can't I know what you're doing? I'm your sister."

George moved over to Maggie and put his arm around her narrow shoulders. "It's hard to explain, Maggie, it's not because we don't like you, it's just...secret, that's all."

George didn't think that he was giving a very good explanation but was afraid of giving away too many details. He really did feel sorry for his sister but she had such a big mouth and a big mouth was a serious problem when it came to George and Charlie's plans.

"I promise I won't tell," Maggie said sincerely, her over-large blue eyes rimmed with red.

George sat in silence, thinking for a moment. *Would it really hurt to tell Maggie?* He knew that she hadn't made any good friends yet because she was too shy to approach the girls her age. Maybe he should tell his sister and give her something to get excited about; after all, he was her big brother.

"Okay, Maggie, we'll let you in on the secret, but you have to promise me that you won't tell anyone what we tell you; it's really important."

Maggie's eyes lit up happily as she nodded and followed George back to his room practically jumping with excitement.

Charlie met George's eye with a wary look when he saw Maggie enter the room with him.

"Okay, Charlie, I think we should tell her. She's promised that she won't tell...I trust her."

Charlie's tense expression softened and he smiled at Maggie. "Okay, explain away then, George. You may want to take a seat for this, Maggie."

Maggie listened to George's story with a look of intense concentration on her face. She listened to the story of the two families who disappeared and how the boys had discovered the names of the two families, Redwin and Regale. She learned what had happened to George and Charlie on the peak of Mount Dusk and that now they had new evidence straight from Uncle Hubert's forbidden study.

"Wow," Maggie breathed in awe. "So I actually did see that face on the tree...I told you so."

George laughed and looked expectantly at Charlie, "So are we going to look through these papers or not?"

Charlie pulled the papers out from under the bed and the three friends gathered around them as if they were made of fire and it was a cold day.

"I haven't actually looked at the papers," Charlie said, while reading over what looked like an old budget. "I just grabbed papers that hadn't been looked at in a while so that Uncle Hubert wouldn't notice that they were missing."

The papers were mostly just random business scribbles or math sums that they cast aside.

"Hey, what's this?" Maggie asked, handing the piece of paper she was holding to George.

George took the yellow old paper and studied it.

One quart. cup of tree matter

Two hairs of the 'object'

A sample of skin from the 'object'

One quart. cup of ground matter

Place all 'object' matter in your ritual

bowl. Over the bowl recite "He of 'object', he of enemy, may you be cast where my desire's lie."

Place tree matter into bowl. Over the bowl recite "I curse you to be, I curse you to stay."

Place ground matter into bowl. Over the bowl recite "Here you are rooted, here eternally you shall lie"

Bury all bowl matter in your curse destination. Over burial site recite "My will be done."

George's hands shook as he finished reading the old paper. He wordlessly handed it over to Charlie. As Charlie read, his eyes widened and an appalled look covered his face.

"What is it?" Maggie asked, nonplussed

"It's a spell, Maggie," Charlie said in a very serious voice, "and a terrible one at that."

George nodded his agreement. "I think we can safely say now that the Regales certainly did disappear, but they never left the town."

"Just think," Charlie said quietly, staring at the spell. "This piece of paper destroyed the lives of the Regales. I can't believe that someone actually cursed those people. If we don't help them who knows how long they'll stay there, unable to move, with only their bad memories for company."

The three of them were quiet for a moment, each feeling very sorry for the poor Regales. George, Maggie and Charlie stayed in the bedroom going over details of the mystery until Maggie was called to go to bed. Maggie reluctantly left and George doubted that she would fall asleep any time soon. He could just picture her sitting in her pink bed telling her teddy about all that had happened. Maggie strongly denied that she ever spoke to "Teddles" but George had caught her many times before. Charlie looked at the time and said he had to go home and return the papers but George made sure that he copied down the sinister spell before it was taken away.

XXX

The next day George, Charlie and Maggie walked to school, whispering the whole way about their mystery. As they were walking, they passed the path that led to the peak of Mount Dusk. George stared up at the mountain, imagining the poor Regale family confined to their bark prisons. He must make a trip up there again soon, he thought to himself. *But alone this time.* He had to talk to them for as long as he could without anyone panicking, so he could learn more about them and their terrible fate. But as much as George was brave he couldn't help but be scared at the prospect of going back up to the peak of Mount Dusk again. It had been a terrifying experience the first time. What would the second time be like?

The two boys and Maggie entered school and separated to go to their different classrooms, promising to find each other at lunch.

George and Charlie sat down in their usual seats. George was just unpacking his pencil case and exercise book when he noticed something out of the corner of his eye. Yvonne was staring at him with—what was it? Curiosity? When George looked up, Yvonne flushed profusely and turned around in her seat to face the front again, her usual scowl back in place. George sat there, considering what had just happened. He had only ever encountered contempt from Yvonne and he found himself inexplicably happy that she had just looked on him in such a way. George carefully probed his feelings. Did he like Yvonne? No, certainly not! She was a snobby, mean girl, not to mention his best friend's sister. Then why did George suddenly find himself smiling stupidly and stealing glances at the black-haired beauty? Unsettled, he tried to put his mind to other things. He opened his history book *The Mysterious Mount Dusk* and started flipping through it, searching for something to take his mind off Yvonne and her strange looks. *Girls,* George thought to himself. *Why do they have to be so unpredictable? Maybe my next mystery can be girls and why they have to confuse boys with strange looks.*

"Good morning, class!" Came the familiar singsong voice of Miss Roland as she swept into the classroom, a smile on her pleasant face as she sprayed the potted plant on her desk just like any other morning. They all chanted, "Good morning" back and went through the morning roll call.

The morning passed quickly as they did sums for math and took notes on natural disasters. It struck George that there was a distinct similarity between Yvonne and a hurricane. One minute you know your surroundings by heart; the next you're upside down, feeling dizzy. George laughed to himself and blushed when Charlie asked why he was smiling so much. When the lunch bell rang, George and Charlie packed up their belongings and made their way to find Maggie. They went to her classroom but it was empty. So they went out into the gardens to find her, but she wasn't there.

"Where is she?" George asked, annoyed that he was wasting his lunch time wandering around in search of his sister.

"I don't know. Let's go and sit under the tree we always do; she can find us there." Charlie suggested and they made their way to their favorite tree.

It was a beautiful tree; a large willow that bordered on the side of a little creek that ran through the school grounds. The lovely hanging branches with their delicate leaf covering acted as a kind of curtain, separating them from the rest of the students. After twenty minutes of idle chat, they were interrupted by an out-of-breath Maggie.

"You'll...never...guess what...I just...heard," She gasped, fighting for breath and pressing a stitch in her side.

The boys both directed their attention to Maggie as she settled herself in front of them, brimming with excitement.

"Where have you been?" George asked impatiently, wishing his sister would hurry up and give an explanation for her strange behavior.

"I've been spying on Miss Roland," Maggie said with her breath back. Here she paused dramatically, teasing George and Charlie with her secret knowledge.

"And?" George prompted, getting even more annoyed.

"Well, I had to return books to the library after class and I went back to your classroom to find you guys; I thought you may have waited for me there."

Here she paused again, relishing knowing something that her brother did not.

"When I heard Miss Roland talking, I thought at first that she must be talking to a student, so I waited just outside the door for her to finish, but I soon found out that she was not talking to a student, she was talking to her potted plant!"

George and Charlie looked at each other, puzzled but intrigued.

"Well, go on! Tell us what she was saying!" Charlie prompted.

"Okay," Maggie started again. "I'd peeked around the door and saw the plant. At first I thought that she was just crazy and then….the plant spoke back!"

George gasped in shock. "Oh, she must have taken a plant from the peak of Mount Dusk…why did she go there, I wonder."

"I'm getting to that," Maggie squealed excitedly. "As I listened, I heard the plant say, 'Go, our great-great grandchild, save yourself; there is nothing to be done for us.' And Miss Roland replied, 'Never! I am your last kinswoman and the only one who can help. I only wish that Hubert Redwin was not watching me so closely. He uses horrible methods of spying on me. But one day I shall overpower him and save you all. If I don't, who will? And then I can finally use my true name—Patricia Regale.' She is a Regale!"

George and Charlie sat stunned for a whole minute, processing this new information.

"So that conversation between Yvonne and Miss Roland on my first day..." George pondered aloud, the wheels in his brain turning.

"Yvonne must know!" Charlie surmised for him. "I wonder how much she knows. She can't know the full story or I don't think that Miss Roland would dare put one of her ancestors in the classroom disguised as a plant...I wonder what Uncle Hubert has told her?"

The three of them pondered aloud for the rest of lunch but came to no new conclusions, just more questions. How was Uncle Hubert spying on Miss Roland? What did Yvonne know? Did Miss Roland have a plan for her trapped family? How did the Regale bloodline survive?

As they all talked George realized that there was only one thing he could do to get sufficient answers; he must talk to the Regales himself, and that's what he would do at the first given opportunity.

CHAPTER 6

Circus Family

*T*he weekend came with sunshine and a hint of spring in the air. Anyone passing a lawn would breathe in deeply the enticing scent of freshly-cut grass. Plants sprouted buds and tiny little birds *pip*ped as they bounced along under the trees. George and Charlie were sitting under their favorite willow tree after school on Friday afternoon, discussing what they could do with their free time. Maggie was at home; she had been absent from school that with a head cold and so the two boys made their plans without her.

"Hmmm, maybe we should have a sleep-over," George said lazily, as he dragged a long stick through the water of the creek.

"Yeah, good idea," Charlie yawned back. "Will your mum mind if I stay over?"

"Well, Maggie's sick, so your house it is!" George replied with a sneaky grin on his face.

"Oh fine, but we're not investigating tonight," Charlie said sharply, giving is friend a knowing look. "We'll watch movies but under no circumstances are we going into Uncle Hubert's study. We should give it a rest for a little while; play it safe for once, alright?"

"Hmmm," George said, not committing himself to a reply.

The two boys started walking to George's house so that he could ask his mother if he could sleep at Charlie's and get some clothes. Once again, George found himself staring up at the peak of Mount Dusk and getting goose bumps at the thought of what was up there. He knew that he wouldn't be able to put off revisiting the Regales for much longer.

The boys reached the Mutton residence and found Mrs. Mutton in the front garden trying to bend over and pick the first flower to bloom. George ran over and picked it for her, for she was far too pregnant to reach for herself.

"Oh, thank you, dear!" Mrs. Mutton said, affectionately cupping George's face with her free hand.

"No worries, Mum," George replied. "Can I sleep at Charlie's tonight, please?"

George's mum started to say yes but then stopped.

"You know, I haven't even met Charlie's uncle. It would be pretty irresponsible for me to let you go without meeting him. I know you've already stayed there, but I think that was a mistake. How about I drop you and Charlie off and meet Mr. Redwin at the same time?"

George and Charlie threw quick glances of panic to each other. What would George's mum say when she met the formidable Mr. Redwin? But they had no choice. If George wanted to stay over he was going to have to let his mum meet Uncle Hubert. So George got some clothes together and the two boys and Mrs. Mutton loaded into the family station wagon. George had no idea how his mother was managing to drive with her large tummy in the way but he kept his thought to himself. His mother was a bit touchy on how big she was. *If Uncle Hubert's mean to Mum then she won't let me stay*, George silently panicked in the back seat. *For once I hope he can manage a smile.*

The car pulled into the drive way and George's mum let out a gasp.

"My goodness!" she exclaimed. "No wonder you want to stay here, George!"

They all trooped up to the front door and Charlie knocked. Rosemary opened the door and smiled at every one.

"Hello, Charlie and George," she said messing the two boys' hair affectionately. "And you must be Mrs. Mutton—charmed." Rosemary curtsied to George's mum, who looked thoroughly confused at the royal treatment.

"Oh, ah, yes I am. I just came to meet Mr. Redwin, as the boys have planned a sleep-over."

Rosemary's smiled faltered for a second. She obviously harbored the same fears as George and Charlie. Was Uncle Hubert going to be mean? Rosemary led them into the massive entrance hall and hurried upstairs to rouse Uncle Hubert. Mrs. Mutton looked around, taking in the rich surroundings with little exclamations of delight.

"Oh, what lovely stained glass...Oh, such a soft rug! Gold stairs, can you imagine?"

They stood there for a few minutes. George and Charlie were nervous and shuffling their feet. Then Uncle Hubert appeared at the top of the stairs, nose in the air, back straight and tall he descended the stairs and swooped on Mrs. Mutton, taking her hand and kissing it as he bowed to her.

"Carol, how lovely to meet you at last."

George and Charlie could not have been more shocked if Yvonne had started handing out friendship bracelets. Why on earth was Uncle Hubert being nice?

George's mother blushed and tittered. "Likewise," was all she managed through her giggles. "Is it alright if George stays the night here?" She asked smiling.

Uncle Hubert turned his back on Mrs. Mutton and faced the two boys, his usual cold look covering his features once more. "Of course," he replied, turning to smile at George's mum again.

"Well then, have a good time, boys; I see my worries had absolutely no basis." And with that, George's mum waddled out of the Redwin castle, still blushing.

"It always helps," Uncle Hubert started grinning at the boys' shocked faces, "to have a little trust in your town."

XXX

The night flew by with the usual spectacular dinner of delicately roasted food made by Rosemary, scary movies and some smuggled potato chips and chocolate bars. George was starting to feel sleepy and about to suggest turning in for the night when the faint sound of the front doors closing started George thinking of a very daring, or perhaps very stupid, plan.

"Charlie, I want to know where your uncle goes every night."

Charlie laughed "Yeah but the only way to find that out is to follow...George, no! I hope you aren't suggesting that we follow my uncle."

George grinned and ran to put his jacket on.

"Quick! Before he gets out of sight."

Charlie groaned but hurriedly pulled on his jacket too. The boys quietly crept down the stairs, trying desperately not to make a sound, and ran to the front doors. They had to slip out before a wandering Rosemary or Yvonne caught them. As soon as George was outside, he questioned his impulsive decision to chase Charlie's uncle. He would hate to be the cause of a family feud; the last thing Charlie needed was to give his family reason to treat him worse. But one thought of the poor Regale family, including his lovely teacher, was enough to make him run down the sloping lawns of the towering Redwin residence.

The crisp night air was cold on George's ears; he pulled his jacket hood onto his head to protect himself not only from the cold but Uncle Hubert's piercing gaze. Charlie followed suit. George could just make out a billowing black cloak rounding the end of the street. The boys ran after Uncle Hubert, scared of losing him. They kept close to the shadows, always keeping Uncle Hubert only just in sight in case he decided to turn around. But Uncle Hubert did not turn around; he walked quickly and purposefully, looking straight ahead.

After fifteen minutes of following him, the two boys came to a stop, trying to catch their breath quietly. They could see Uncle Hubert standing on somebody's front lawn. The house was secluded and large with a charming garden of little flowers. It was the only house on the last street at the edge of town. George and Charlie watched as the front door of the house opened and out came Miss Roland.

"Stop, Hubert! I cannot take another night of this insanity! Just leave me be!" Miss Roland cried, her eyes pleading with Uncle Hubert.

George felt a pang in his chest as he looked at his pretty teacher's tense face and sad eyes.

Uncle Hubert watched Miss Roland for a few moments with a small smile playing on his lips. Then he raised his hand to the sky.

"Redwin Guards, I call thee!" He hollered, his smile growing larger and finally meeting his cold eyes.

Two balls of mist suddenly appeared on the lawn of Miss Roland's house. Miss Roland started to sob in terror and ran back into her house. George heard a series of locks click and saw Miss Roland hurriedly shut the curtains; he could still hear her wailing.

The two balls of mist started to take shape. One grew tall; it stayed a swirling mass of dim color for a few moments and then took the shape of a man. The other shorter one took the shape of a woman. Heads first, they started to appear. The man had a handlebar moustache, a festive maroon vest edged in gold, and, as George and Charlie looked on in horror, they realized that where his legs should join to his torso a unicycle started to form. The man had no legs—he was half man, half unicycle. The woman had unruly black hair flowing down her back; her eyes were covered with an elaborate gold and jeweled mask and her lips were painted deep crimson. She wore a long old-fashioned black dress that trailed along the ground.

The two slightly transparent guards started to slowly drift around the lawn, always facing Miss Roland's house.

"Keep her here, my dearest ancestors," Uncle Hubert called to the horrific apparitions as he turned on his heel and started to walk back down the street, right towards George and Charlie who were concealed behind a bush.

George and Charlie faced each other, terror in their eyes.

"We have to make it back to my bedroom before Uncle Hubert gets to the front doors!" Charlie squealed, throat constricted with panic. "Oh, why did we do this? I don't want to know!"

The two boys sat still waiting for Uncle Hubert to pass them. It was too late to hope to get out in front of him in time. He was nearly upon them, when George had the insane feeling that he was about to giggle. Choking down his panic, he saw Uncle Hubert pass them in a swirl of black. The two boys looked at each other, then silently crept from their hiding place. Hearts in their mouths, they started to cut across lawns, as fast as they dared, trying to take a shortcut to Charlie's house. As the boys ran, a deadly wave of hatred burned in George's mind. *He's pure evil*, George thought to himself as he pounded across town. *This has to end*. After a few minutes of frenzied running and leaping they were ahead of Uncle Hubert, but only just. George realized that they were never going to make it to Charlie's bedroom before Uncle Hubert reached the front doors but a new plan was already forming in George's mind which was oddly clear and calm.

The two boys made the last sprint to Charlie's front doors with their breath burning in their lungs and knew that it was only a matter of seconds before Uncle Hubert rounded the corner and spotted them.

"Charlie, pretend to be sick," George whispered urgently.

Charlie didn't even need to be asked to pretend. He promptly threw up on the immaculate lawns in front of the Redwin castle just as Uncle Hubert rounded the corner. He caught sight of the two boys and broke in to a run.

"What have you two been doing!" he thundered, looking murderous, his nostrils flaring ominously.

George swallowed hard, meeting the small hateful little eyes of Uncle Hubert and tried to force a sincere smile on his face.

"Ch...Charlie felt sick, sir, so...so we came outside for some fresh air."

Uncle Hubert looked at his nephew suspiciously. "You have not left these grounds tonight, have you?" He asked, his eyes boring into George's.

"No, sir," George replied, trying to sound innocent, "of course not."

Seeming satisfied with the explanation, Uncle Hubert nodded curtly.

"Charlie, go to Rosemary. She will treat your illness." And with that Uncle Hubert swept indoors, closing the front door behind him.

"I didn't know you were really sick!" George exclaimed, relieved that his plan had worked.

"I'm not sick," Charlie replied shakily. "I just got so nervous that I threw up."

The two boys stared at each other for a moment and then burst out in hysterical giggles, collapsing with relief that their great adventure was over for the night.

xxx

The two friends lay in Charlie's bed re-capping their mind-blowing adventure. "Poor Miss Roland," Charlie muttered, his voice muffled with lethargy.

"She's really Miss Regale," George pointed out, trying to erase the image of his teacher's stricken face from his mind.

He hated knowing that right at this moment she was probably sobbing, terrified out of her wits.

"I hope we can help her."

George closed his eyes for a moment, trying to think of how they could possibly eradicate Miss Roland's ghostly captors from the town. It seemed hopeless; George and Charlie couldn't do magic like Uncle Hubert. When he opened his eyes he was surprised to see Charlie sitting up facing him. Charlie's face was glowing red with anger and his fists were clenched.

"I am so ashamed!" He declared, voice quavering with emotion. "It's my family, my own flesh and blood who are doing this to her. But I swear, I swear that I will redeem my family name and free the Regale family if it's the last thing I do."

George put a hand on his friend's shoulder and gently pushed him back down on the bed.

"I know you will, mate, and I'm with you all the way. Let's just try and think of a solution now. Do you think that perhaps your uncle has a book of spells, Charlie?"

Charlie thought for a moment. "Yes, I'd say he would—some sacred Redwin book of All-Things-Horrible."

"Well, then, I think our next move should be to find that book. Even if there isn't some form of counter-curse in there, at least Uncle Hubert won't have access to any more dreadful curses."

CHAPTER 7

The Book

George was getting frustrated. His mother had forced him to come straight home from school on Monday for some "family time" when he had been planning to help Charlie forage through his uncle's study. Maggie was helping Mrs. Mutton cook dinner and George's job was to deck the dining table out with their finest cutlery, candles and tablecloth.

"Done!" George called moodily from the dining room.

Mrs. Mutton bustled in and clucked her tongue. "You didn't even iron the tablecloth!" She scolded, wagging her finger at George. "You'll have to start again; off you go."

George bit his tongue to stop himself from rudely replying: "As you wish, Your Majesty." Half an hour later the dinner was done, the table was set and the whole family was seated in front of a delicious meal of chicken and mushroom pie.

"Ah, isn't this nice?" George's dad said happily looking around the table, "Except, of course, for George's face. Swallowed a lemon, George?"

George tried to relax his features into a smile. "Sorry, Dad, just a bit tired. How's work?"

"Oh well, it's a lot of fun, although the funny bloke down the street keeps telling me I'm a hazard to anything breakable; don't know what he means by it, funny guy." The rest of the family hid giggles; it was well known that Mr. Mutton was incredibly clumsy.

"How's school, kids?" He asked, smiling warmly at his two children.

"Completely normal," George and Maggie replied in unison.

Mrs. Mutton looked at them suspiciously. "'Normal?' What kind of an answer is that?"

George and Maggie looked at each other. They shuddered to think of what would happen if their parents found out about the mystery surrounding George's teacher. They would probably move to the other side of the planet. *Time for a diversion tactic*, George thought to himself.

"How are you feeling, Mum—the twins feeling healthy?"

George's Mum positively glowed at being asked about the babies. "Oh yes, they're happily kicking away, the little cuties."

George didn't know how she could possibly know if the babies were cute or not, considering that no one could see them. Mr. Mutton reached for his wife's hand and they gazed at each other lovingly for a moment until George and Maggie started to protest about feeling sick at the sight of them.

xxx

Later that night as George lay in bed listening to the comforting sound of the night wind whistling through the trees his thoughts once again turned to the horrible fate of the Regales. George felt slightly ashamed of himself for abandoning the Regales up there on that mountain top all alone; he had been planning to revisit them but fear had kept him at bay. *Not anymore*, George thought to himself, *they must need some form of company.*

George quickly jumped out of bed and dressed quietly. He knew that Charlie and Maggie would be upset that he had not waited for them to come along, too, but George felt that this was something he should do alone and he planned to keep this night time adventure his little secret to spare their feelings.

George started to creep down the hallway when a small movement caught his eye. The stained glass portrait of the crying Regale man had lifted his head and was smiling at George. George had to shove his fist in his mouth to keep from crying out in shock. As he looked at the portrait he had a sudden thought.

"Thomas Regale?" George whispered to the portrait.

Slowly the portrait gave a small nod.

"I was just going to speak to you on the mountain, I have questions and I need some answers."

The portrait nodded again, then resumed its usual sullen pose.

xxx

George reached the peak of Mount Dusk puffing, his breath coming out in bursts of frosted white in front of his face. He was still very shaken by the encounter with the window. It's not every day a window smiles at you, or a tree for that matter. Everything in the Mount Dusk mystery was so strange that sometimes George wished he had never started the investigation, wished that he could be a normal boy riding a bike to school and never giving a second thought to trees with souls or ghostly guards terrorizing his teacher. But here he was seeking out the mystery once more in the cold. He wandered around trying to find the place where the Regale family were trapped. After ten minutes of fruitless searching with his hands smarting from the relentless cold night air he stopped and sat down, frustrated with himself for not remembering where the Regales were. Just as George was about to give up and go home to his comfortable, and especially warm, bed he heard a familiar long moan on the breeze.

"Chiiild. Come."

George stood up and ran through the trees, following the eerie voice that was calling to him until he finally found the tall cluster of Regales. Only one tree had its face on tonight.

George walked up to Thomas Regale slightly fearful, no matter how good he knew the Regales to be. It was scary being in a dark wood seeing the moonlight play tricks with its friend the shadow.

"I didn't know that you could visit my house," he mumbled feeling unsure of himself.

How do you act around a haunted tree?

"It was a precaution that my family took when we sensed that Redwin was up to no good," Thomas Regale said in a rush.

George realized that he had probably waited centuries to tell somebody his story.

"We trapped part of our souls in the windows of our house with the help of one Redwin and her namesake spell book. We thought that this way we could summon help quickly if one of us should perish but, alas, nobody has lived in that house since we left it—nobody that is until you arrived in town."

George mulled over the story thoughtfully.

"A Redwin helped you?" he asked finally.

"Yes. A Miss Catherine Redwin who I suspect is the great-great-great grandmother of your little friend. They seem to share the same sense of goodness that is rare in their bloodline."

"So there *is* a spell book! A Redwin spell book." George said, elated that his theory had been correct.

"Yes, and it is our only chance of salvation from this cursed fate."

George smiled at Thomas. "Don't worry, Mister Regale, I'll find the spell to free you and use it at once."

"No you won't. Only a Redwin may use the Redwin spells," Thomas said sadly. "We learned that the hard way. When Catherine helped us gain the spell book she didn't know that it was useless to us. Confident that we had a way to defeat Redwin, we confronted him, chanting one of his own spells. It did nothing and he turned around, ready to curse us into the damp ground." Thomas Regale's voice was filled with bitter resentment that had been festering for centuries.

After they had been talking for a few hours, the sky slowly started to lighten and George bid Thomas goodbye. Thomas Regale had insisted on George giving a detailed explanation of what the town was like now and what the current Redwins did with themselves. Thomas was very sad to hear that the Redwin ghosts—people he had known when they were living—were harassing Miss Roland.

"The female ghost is Millicent Redwin; she was a performer in the Redwin circus in my day with her husband Philip Redwin, the unicyclist. My poor great-great-great grandchild is being haunted by those despicable characters and I can't help her," he had said with a terrible sadness thickening his words.

George hurried down the mountain until he reached his house. He hadn't meant to be up the mountain as long as he had been and he was exhausted with fatigue and the excitement of talking to the famous Regales. As he sneaked through the front door, a furious voice shattered the early morning silence.

"Oh, look who decided to pop in, dear."

Mr. and Mrs. Mutton were seated at the dining table looking mutinous. George's blood froze and his heart seemed to stop. He was in very big trouble.

XXX

George's punishment was severe; no television, no sleep-overs, no dessert and all of Maggie's chores were his for two weeks. Mrs. Mutton had screeched at George that his parents had been worried sick and what did he think he was doing sneaking out and at such an hour? George couldn't tell them the truth for fear of being whisked out of town, so he had told them that he was just seeing what the town was like at night. George didn't like lying to his parents but there were people's lives and souls in danger. As if this wasn't punishment enough, Charlie and Maggie stopped talking to him. They had been appalled to think that George had gone on an adventure without them; after all of the effort they had all put in, George had been selfish enough to deprive them of the night's excitement.

"Your problem, George," Charlie had basically spat at him, "is that you refuse to be a team player. You just have to be leader, don't you? Great courageous George is just out for himself. Who do you think you are?"

George had never felt worse in his whole life. The mystery was put on hold, he had no friends and didn't even have movies to distract himself. Not that he had any time for movies with all the extra chores he was doing. After a week of being wracked with guilt and self-pity, he was relieved when Charlie and Maggie finally approached him. George was sitting under a willow tree at lunchtime when his angry friend and sister walked up to him with curiously satisfied smirks pulling at their mouths.

"We have some news for you," Charlie said in an infuriatingly superior tone that made George want to tell him to go away.

"Since," Maggie carried on, "you saw fit to exclude us from part of the investigation..." Here she stopped talking and glared at George for a moment. "...we have done the same and now we are even."

George stared at them for a few moments, caught between feelings of indignation and curiosity.

"Okay," George said, giving in to his curiosity "we'll compare stories but then we're even and you can't be angry at me anymore."

Charlie and Maggie laughed and sat down next to George.

"You first," Charlie said, slapping him on the back.

George recapped his most recent visit to Mount Dusk for them, feeling happy that he finally was telling someone. Charlie and Maggie were an intent audience, gasping in all of the right parts of the story. When he had finished, George quickly requested their new information in return. Charlie smiled and looked very pleased with himself.

"Without further ado," he reached into his bag, "I give you the Redwin Family Book of Horror!"

Charlie pulled a very old book from his bag. It had a worn brown leather cover that seemed to be emitting a faint red glow. George stared in shock at the old book.

"That's not...I mean—wow! Charlie, how did you get it?"

"Well now, that's an interesting story, isn't it, Maggie?"

Maggie nodded enthusiastically, smiling triumphantly.

"The night that I found out you had gone up that mountain, I was angry, George—really angry—so I put in a secret call to Maggie and had her meet me the next day at my house. I was really just planning to vent my anger with her but a very rare thing happened. When Maggie knocked on the front door, Yvonne answered...Maggie, please take over."

Charlie and Maggie looked at each other, grinning.

"No worries, Charlie. Well, I was a little afraid that Yvonne was going to be mean to me so I didn't at first say why I had come over; I knew she'd treat me badly if she knew I was Charlie's friend, but she just assumed that I wanted to see her, us both being girls and all, I'm guessing."

Maggie smiled at George but he was completely nonplussed. "So...you're friends with Yvonne now?" George fleetingly remembered that funny look Yvonne had given him in class and a flush erupted on his cheeks when he said her name.

"That's right, well done, George! Now, can you guess why that's a good thing?" Maggie asked, once again using her secret knowledge to her pride's advantage.

George sat silently for a moment, thinking. *What is so great about my sister being friends with a mean person who is siding with that maniac Uncle Hubert?* And then it clicked.

"She will confide in you! She'll let you in on some of what

she knows about Uncle Hubert. But I still don't understand how some girly chat got you the spell book."

Here Charlie resumed the story.

"Don't you see, George? Yvonne's a girl and what do girls like to do best? Chat! Yvonne has had absolutely no one to blab Uncle Hubert's secrets to. She certainly hasn't told her little red-haired friend whose family is really rich; the girl's parents would hit the roof if they knew. So Yvonne's been bursting to tell someone and who should knock on the door? A girl who she'd seen at school who has no friends. With the way that Yvonne's mind works she would think Maggie would never tell a soul her secrets in case she lost her only friend. So she told Maggie almost everything she knew about Uncle Hubert. Including where the spell book was."

George sat stunned. Maggie was friends with Yvonne, they had the Redwin spell book and...*and now Yvonne might come to my house to visit Maggie,* a sly voice added in George's mind. All round the news was great and the three investigators sat smiling and laughing at their good fortune.

xxx

George and Charlie were sitting in George's room looking through Uncle Hubert's spell book before dinner. George was in high spirits now that he had his best friend back. It had been awful feeling so guilty about upsetting Charlie and Maggie but now everything was back to normal.

Some spells in the book were even worse than George had previously feared. There was one particularly gruesome one called "Limb Twistation" which had a diagram of a man whose arms and legs were mangled. By the time they had read to the end of the book George was feeling slightly ill. It was inconceivable that any human being could be so evil as to use these spells on any one—but there was one such person: Uncle Hubert.

Maggie was having dinner at the Redwin residence tonight

and George couldn't help but admire his sister for being so brave as to walk in there trying to dig up more information when she was only seven. For as long as George could remember, he had fought with Maggie, but, now that they were sharing a common goal, they were thick as thieves.

The boys found the counter-curse to the Regales misfortune on the very last page of the spell book.

"This is it." George said, quietly marveling at how he was holding the key to the Regale's freedom in his very hands.

Charlie took the book and stared at the page for a few minutes. "So this is what I've got to learn to do."

George was momentarily stunned until he realized what Charlie meant. "Oh wow, you're a Redwin, so can you use these spells!"

"Well spotted, professor," Charlie laughed. "You never put it together that I was a Redwin and only Redwins can use these spells?"

Charlie and George laughed at the slip of mind (George secretly feeling rather embarrassed.)

"We'll start with something simple," George said. "The one at the start of the book to make a rosebud bloom seems like the easiest."

They looked at the rosebud spell and were trying to memorize it when they were interrupted by the call for dinner. Dinner was the usual delicious happy affair until they were interrupted by a strange noise—horse hoof-beats.

"Oh no," Charlie moaned softly, putting his head in his hands. "How embarrassing."

George rushed to the front door and pulled it open. An old-fashioned horse-drawn carriage was pulled up at the front of his house. Seated in the carriage were Yvonne and Maggie. Neither of them had spotted George because they were having a heated argument.

"How dare you! I thought we could be friends; I thought that you could be trusted, more importantly," Yvonne cried out into the night.

"But Yvonne, people's souls are in danger. Oh please, don't tell on me, please, Yvonne?" Maggie's little voice was thick with tears.

"I won't tell because...well, I haven't decided what I think on the matter. I'm confused, which is why I was so glad to have you to confide in. But if I can't trust you, then there's no point to being friends. Goodbye, Maggie."

Maggie jumped out of the carriage, crying hard into her jumper and George ran out to meet her. Before the carriage had a chance to get down the driveway, Yvonne and George's eyes met. Yvonne looked sadly at him for a moment then lowered her head and the carriage trotted off back down the street.

"Maggie, what's wrong?" George asked but he already knew the answer.

"She...she caught me," Maggie said haltingly through her tears. "I was sneaking into the study after saying that I needed the bathroom and she jumped out from around the corner. I think she suspected me, so she followed me. Oh, poor Yvonne! She's really nice when you get to know her and now she's in that big house with that horrible uncle of hers telling her what to do. Oh George, I'm so sorry!"

Maggie buried her head in George's shoulder, her little frame shaking with sobs. George felt infinitely sorry for his little sister and very guilty too. Maggie was so keen to please George that she had put herself at risk. George thought to himself that, being her older brother, he shouldn't have let her go. It was unfair to say the least.

"You did great, Maggie, and, don't worry, one day Yvonne will understand why we have to do this, I'm sure. You just go inside and wash your face. You did your best and that's all anyone can ask of you."

Maggie walked inside and George heard her tell their mother that she and Yvonne had got into an argument over a missing lip-gloss.

Charlie wandered outside looking worried.

"What's wrong with Maggie?"

"Take a guess." George answered heavily. "Your family has a horse-drawn carriage?" George added, smirking.

Charlie reddened.

"Yeah, it's been in my family for ages, apparently, and Uncle Hubert refuses to acknowledge technology. He says it's against tradition."

"Do you think Yvonne is growing less fond of your family traditions?" George asked.

He had more than just one reason to want that to be true—not that he ever wanted Charlie to find that out.

"She certainly has surprised me. I've always seen her as, well, a cow but she seemed to be acting nice towards Maggie, which is close to a miracle."

The two boys sat down on the front porch, staring unseeing at the front garden.

"Charlie, are you getting a little bit scared?" George asked quietly.

"George, I've been scared this whole time." Charlie answered seriously "For my whole life I've been scared of my uncle, scared of Matty and Billy, scared of Yvonne and now what I'm scared of is what's going to happen to us if we're caught. I don't know what it feels like just to be plain old comfortable."

George stared at his friend, feeling the heavy weight of pity in his chest. He always knew that Charlie was quiet and reserved but he had never really put it down to fear—just a general annoyance at his family.

"But one thing that's helping me feel a lot less scared all the time is this mystery, George." Charlie carried on a bit louder "Before all of this, I never would have dreamed of invading Uncle Hubert's study or sneaking out at night or even...talking to someone like you."

Here Charlie looked at George and smiled.

"It's all changing. I'm not scared of Matty and Billy anymore; they're just idiots. I'm not scared of Yvonne; she's just as scared of Uncle Hubert as I am. I'm sure of it. And I'm slowly starting to not be scared of Uncle Hubert, because we're beating him, George, beating him at his own game."

"Yeah, we are," George replied, slapping his friend on the back. "Now let's go practice that rose spell and make a proper Redwin out of you."

The two boys laughed and made their way back inside the house.

CHAPTER 8

Yvonne

*T*he signs of Maggie and Yvonne's broken friendship were very noticeable at school. Although Yvonne was always cold to everyone, she was particularly so towards Maggie and as a result Maggie was constantly on the verge of tears. Charlie looked on at this with some concern. George was positive that Charlie had been hoping to see a change in Yvonne, perhaps even to see Yvonne on their side fighting Uncle Hubert.

But now it seemed all chances of that were off. Yvonne stalked past them in the halls with her head held high and her nose in the air. She giggled with her red-haired friend whenever Maggie was in sight and George had never seen Maggie look so miserable.

After a few days of this cruel treatment Charlie made a peculiar suggestion to Maggie as they sat under their favorite willow tree at lunchtime.

"Go and talk to her."

George and Maggie looked at Charlie in amazement.

"Are you crazy?" Maggie asked incredulously. "She'd just reject me and then I'd feel even worse. No way."

"I don't think so," Charlie replied "I've known Yvonne her entire life and out of all that time I have never seen her be so nice to anyone as she was to you. I think she genuinely likes you and if anyone has a chance of befriending her, it's you."

Maggie thought carefully about this, biting her lip.

"Well, when you put it like that, it seems possible. And I would like to stop crying every day."

"So do it already! I haven't had any luck with those Redwin spells, so if we can recruit another Redwin to try and help us, it can only be a good thing."

Maggie looked curiously at Charlie. "But Charlie, even if she would be my friend again, I doubt I could get her to help us. I mean, no offence, but she seems to hate you, so why would she help you?"

Charlie grimaced "Yeah, you're probably right—but it's worth a shot at least. Try talking to her when she's on her way home after school and that friend of hers—I think her name's Trinity—won't be there."

Maggie nodded her nervous agreement as the bell for class rang.

The two boys entered their classroom and slumped down in their usual seats. George always felt less attentive after lunch and he yawned widely, stretching his arms out over Charlie's head.

Matty turned around in his seat and, leaning back in his chair, took hold of George's pen.

"Give us a lend, George," he said, letting his seat fall back into its usual place with a dull laugh.

"Hey, give it back!" George yelled making a misjudged snatch for the pen.

Matty held the pen up high with his long, thick arm.

"I dare you to try to get it, Georgina." He said laughing harder now.

George stood up. He was no match for Matty's strength

but he wasn't about to sit down and let Matty take something that belonged to him.

"I said give it back now," George said quietly feeling himself flush with anger and embarrassment.

He knew Yvonne was watching and the thought of that turned his stomach into knots.

"Oh gee, George, you're so scary. If only I'd known you were going to ask politely for it back then I wouldn't have dared to take your pen."

Matty and Billy laughed, giving each other high fives. George was about to give up and sit down before he was humiliated further, when Charlie stood up next to him.

"He said give it back!" Charlie's voice came strong and filled with hatred.

Everyone in the class looked in shock at Charlie, then in fear at the two blond bullies holding George's pen.

"Oh yeah?" Matty said quietly, glaring at Charlie "And what do you think you're going to do about it, you freak?"

Charlie looked a little frightened but bravely stammered, "Just give it back and I won't have to do anything."

This statement brought gales of laughter not only from Matty and Billy but from Yvonne's friend Trinity too. George looked at Yvonne expecting her to be smirking at her brother's ill treatment, but she wasn't. She was staring at Charlie with a look of deep thought on her face.

"Forget it, freak, the day I'm scared of you is the day George gets a girlfriend."

The two bullies started laughing again, when Yvonne suddenly stood up and grabbed the pen from Matty's hand. She stood still for a few moments looking shocked at what she had just done then threw the pen roughly at George and sat down again with her face glowing. No one knew what to do. Matty and Billy stared at each other, looking even more confused than usual, and George didn't know if he should say thanks or spare Yvonne further embarrassment and shut up.

But nobody looked more stunned than Charlie.

His mouth hung open, as did his eyes as he stared at the back of his sister's head. Just as George decided that he would mutter a "thank you" to Yvonne, Miss Roland walked in and put an end to the business anyway, commenting on how unnaturally silent it was in the classroom.

XXX

After school that day George and Charlie celebrated their victory in standing up to Matty and Billy.

"Did you see his dumb face when Yvonne took the pen? Oh I never want to forget that look." Charlie laughed.

"Well, whenever you feel like you don't remember, just look at a picture of a big ape and that ought to jog your memory."

The two boys laughed even harder as they made their way home.

"George, I don't know about you but I'm feeling pretty good; let's work on the mystery tonight." Charlie smiled at George victory dancing merrily in his eyes.

"Charlie, it's a school night. I doubt either of us will be allowed to stay late at each other's houses."

"This coming from you? The chief of rule breaking? Come on, George, you can do better than that!"

George laughed "Well," he started slowly, "I guess if I told Mum we had a project to do and your uncle has all the encyclopedias for it, she might let me stay 'til nine or something."

The boys made their way to George's house in high spirits. As they walked in the front door they noticed a strange noise, someone breathing heavily mixed with little quiet squeals.

"Hello?" George called, walking through the house to where the noise was coming from.

As the two boys reached George's parents' room they discovered Mrs. Mutton on the bed holding her stomach and emitting the strange noises they had heard previously.

"Mum!" George cried, rushing to her side "What is it? What's wrong?"

"Oh, thank goodness it's you, George. I can't reach the phone. Please call your father and tell him that the twins are coming and fast!"

George raced to the phone while Charlie stood at the bedroom doorway looking awkward. The phone call was made and Mr. Mutton had promised to race home straight away and take his wife to the hospital.

George held his mother's hand the whole time until Mr. Mutton arrived as she squeaked and squealed with the pain of labor. Soon George's parents were on their way to the hospital and George was in charge of looking after Maggie and cooking dinner.

"Baked beans and toast it is!" He declared not having a clue how to cook anything more complicated.

Maggie jumped up and down in excitement when she arrived home and heard the news about her mother.

"This has got to be the best day ever!" she cried. "We're going to have two more brothers, and Yvonne and I are friends again!"

George stopped scooping the baked beans out of the tin and turned to his sister.

"It worked? Are you serious?"

"Yup!" Maggie said skipping around the room "She told me that she has forgiven me on the condition that I never go behind her back again and that I tell her everything I know about Uncle Hubert."

George and Charlie stared at Maggie.

"Are you insane?" George cried, "We don't know if we can trust her! The last I heard she was the enemy! What are we going to do if she decides to turn around and tell Uncle Hubert?"

"Well I think we should give her a chance." Maggie said happily "She's invited us all around this Saturday night to talk it out."

"She invited me to my own house?" Charlie asked, laughing "She really does think a lot of herself."

George thought about it as he popped the pan of beans onto

the stove. Could Yvonne really be trusted? Or did everyone just want to believe that she could? Sighing, George put these questions to his two companions. Both thought that they should give it a shot because they had stopped progressing by themselves. George reluctantly consented to visiting Yvonne on Saturday night; it was not only the thought of the Regale mystery playing on his mind.

xxx

Later that night Mr. Mutton returned home, face glowing with happiness, to tell the children that he was going to stay with their mother in hospital for a couple of days, the babies were healthy and happy and he had acquired Uncle Hubert's promise to look after the Mutton children during their parents' absence. Everyone was shocked to hear the news and Mr. Mutton dropped them off at the Redwin residence on the way to the hospital with a promise to be back in two days, which would be late on Sunday. The three children were fussed over by Rosemary a great deal. Maggie was to sleep in Yvonne's room and George in Charlie's. George was ecstatic at this turn of events. He was to have a two-night sleep-over and was free to investigate Uncle Hubert to his heart's content, which he planned to do as soon as Charlie agreed to it.

Maggie was also very happy; this was a fantastic opportunity to engage Yvonne in the mystery and to have some fun with the only friends she had. Yvonne at first was her usual cold self to George and Charlie but, after spending a couple of hours with Maggie, she consented to enter her brother's room to discuss Uncle Hubert while he was out of the house. Yvonne was scared of Uncle Hubert finding out about her possible switch of alliance and so she declared that she would only discuss the matter in his absence.

Yvonne and Maggie entered Charlie's bedroom looking uncomfortable.

"Hello there," Maggie said bravely, trying to break the uncomfortable silence. "Shall we, err, begin?"

Yvonne stood stiffly by the door making it quite obvious that she had not decided to completely join in yet. George stood and pulled two comfortable looking armchairs across the room for the girls, giving an uncertain smile to Yvonne who blushed faintly but sat down.

"Right," George started, not quite sure what to say, "So we all know why we're here..."

"I don't," Yvonne interrupted, looking peevish "I have no idea what you people know or how you got to know it."

"'You people?'" Charlie asked incredulously. "You mean your brother, your best friend and George, right?"

The twins glared at each other and George was expecting Yvonne to waltz out of the room never to talk to them again but, to George's surprise, Yvonne lowered her head and mumbled her agreement.

"Well...now that that's made things nice and uncomfortable," George said, laughing a little at everyone's pinched faces, "let's start explaining to Yvonne the finer details of our investigation."

George was about to continue when Charlie, who was still studying his sister, called out "Wait! Yvonne hasn't given us much reason to trust her as yet. I think a little contract should be drawn up, just in case."

Yvonne looked daggers at Charlie "Just in case what exactly?"

"Just in case history repeats itself," Charlie said, and George had the feeling that years of rejection by his sister were bubbling up inside his friend.

Everyone was looking at Yvonne now, holding their breath waiting for her answer and, to everyone's dismay, Yvonne quickly got up out of her chair and stalked from the room, followed by a pleading Maggie.

George shook his head and slumped down into the recently-vacated armchair. Now the situation was even more desperate than before. Yvonne now knew that they were up to something and she was angry with them. What was to stop her running to Uncle Hubert? The two boys sat in heavy silence contemplating this horrible outcome when suddenly the bedroom door burst open.

"Uncle Hubert!" The two boys shouted losing their heads.

"No, you fools!" Yvonne spat at them, standing dramatically in the doorway, waving a piece of paper high in the air. "I have written up and signed a contract, witnessed by Maggie here."

Maggie was grinning ear-to-ear, looking very pleased with herself and, as the news slowly sunk into their brains, George and Charlie followed suit. And then, without warning, Yvonne suddenly flew over to Charlie, threw her arms around his neck and kissed his cheek. Everyone was frozen again, except Yvonne who was smiling as George had never seen her smile before, with tears running down her cheeks.

"You have no idea," Yvonne started softly with her voice trembling, "how much I have wanted someone to see the good in me. All these years I have felt so alone with only that horrid old man for company...I just felt too ashamed to ask your forgiveness, Charlie, but now," here she paused to beam at everyone, "but now I have my brother back and two friends to call my own, so I can safely say I am so sorry, Charlie, for never being a proper sister, but sometimes I swear I felt like I was under a spell which kept me at Uncle Hubert's side."

Charlie was gaping at Yvonne, speechless. For many years Yvonne had purposefully ignored, teased and avoided her brother and now here she was shown a chance to make it right and she actually did it.

"It's...err...cool," Charlie stammered. "Let's just get on with the meeting."

Everyone laughed, overjoyed at the twins' reconciliation and the prospect of having the perfect spy.

"Right," George said, "now that...umm...things are sorted we should discuss Uncle Hubert while he's not here."

Everyone nodded their assent, turning serious once more.

"Yvonne, so far we have discovered many disturbing things including a small cluster of trees containing the souls of your family's ancient enemy, the Regale family—and we know that a Redwin trapped them there."

Yvonne gasped and covered her mouth "You can't be serious?" she looked stricken.

"Unfortunately, we are," Charlie answered, tentatively holding her hand.

"Not only that," George continued, "but we have also discovered that Miss Roland is a descendant of the Regales. Judging from your discussion with her on my first day of school, Yvonne, you already know that."

Yvonne slowly shook her head, looking still more mortified. "I did not know that her ancestors were trapped in trees, though! Just that her ancestors and the Redwins were enemies. Oh no, what must she think of me?!"

Yvonne buried her head in Charlie's chest and Charlie, still looking slightly awkward, patted her back soothingly.

"We have also found out that your family spell book is the only way to set the Regales free and we are now in possession of this book."

Here Yvonne perked up a bit. "Uncle Hubert has been teaching me spell-work! I can use the spells!"

Everyone was very happy with this news since Charlie had been failing miserably at them.

"Excellent," George said happily "but it gets worse. Uncle Hubert has the ghosts of your ancestors keeping guard on Miss Roland every night so that she can't help her family. She's terrified of them and we could probably use her help in this. So we need to find a way to dismiss the guards long enough to interrogate Miss Roland. It's too risky talking to her at school, someone might hear us, or worse, Uncle Hubert has a way of watching her at school that we haven't discovered yet."

Here everyone furrowed their brow in deep thought. The

idea of approaching the terrifying Redwin Guards was not a happy one.

"I could try to use magic to dismiss them until you guys have spoken to Miss Roland," Yvonne said in a small voice.

"No way!" Charlie said sternly "It's too dangerous, what if they have some kind of evil powers or they tell Uncle Hubert?"

"Charlie," Yvonne said, softly grasping his hands, "I think I owe something to all of you. You have all been fighting this evil and I have been aiding it. Unless I do you guys a huge favor I'll always feel guilty. So, for the mystery and for my own happiness, please let me do it."

George himself thought that it was a fantastic idea. He too felt that Yvonne owed them something and, with the Redwin spell-work behind her, felt that she would be safer than any of the rest of them in this dreadful task. Charlie looked around at his two Mutton friends and saw that they both agreed with Yvonne. Then slowly he nodded his head, looking very uneasy.

"But we are all to be on watch when Yvonne does it, just in case."

Everyone agreed and, when the front doors creaked open a few minutes later, Yvonne dashed from the room, not wanting Uncle Hubert to catch on to her miraculous change of alliance.

CHAPTER 9

Ben and Bob

On Sunday afternoon Mr. Mutton came to collect George and Maggie to meet their new twin brothers Ben and Bob. When they arrived home, they held their baby brothers, who were tiny and very pink, and kissed their mother who looked very tired. George was extremely happy with his little brothers. After working on a deadly mission for weeks on end, it was wonderful to happily receive two new arrivals into the family. All the babies really did was sleep and drink milk, but they were very cute and made everyone in the house smile when a little sound escaped them or they made a funny face. George and Maggie were given a week off school to properly welcome their brothers into the world but, since they were too young to play, there really wasn't much to do with them. So, instead, the two older children cleaned the house for their mother who needed some sleep and rest. The harmony inside 56 Clover Street made it hard to believe that there was anything wrong with the outside world, but soon enough the week was over and George returned to school, where he was all too aware of the Regale mystery as he was being taught daily by one of the Regales.

Monday morning dawned clear and sunny and the two eldest Mutton children took their time walking to school, enjoying the warm sun on their backs and the delicately flower-scented air. It was a while before either of them noticed the large dark figure on the path in front of them.

"Well well well, hello there, Miss and Mister Mutton."

The two children looked up in surprise at Uncle Hubert. He had on a large, elaborately-embroidered coat that hid his ample stomach.

"Hello, Mister Sir," Maggie squeaked, looking thoroughly nervous.

"I have decided to personally congratulate your parents on their new children," Uncle Hubert said, quietly smirking at the obviously uncomfortable pair.

"Why?" George blurted out before he could stop himself; he was very confused at this awful man's sudden niceness.

"Ah George, is it that unbelievable that I should want to be-friend your parents? As a standing member of the community, I consider it my duty to...bring the townspeople together. One can accomplish much on one's own but it is always better to work as a team; then much, much more can be achieved."

George's blood froze. Uncle Hubert was recruiting his parents!

"Sir, I think they're busy," George said hurriedly, desperate to stop Uncle Hubert in his mission.

"I think I shall continue, anyway." Uncle Hubert said, tiring of the two children "Good day."

Uncle Hubert swept past them and George quickly pulled Maggie the rest of the way to school.

"We have to tell Charlie."

On the school grounds, they found Charlie waiting for them on the front lawn.

"Hey," he started then saw the looks on his friends' faces.

"Oh no, what's happened now?" George and Maggie retold the morning's events hurriedly so that they would not to be interrupted by the school bell.

"Oh, for crying out loud, will it never end?" Charlie burst out unexpectedly. "I mean, at first this whole mystery looked pretty straightforward; set the Regales free. Now on top of evil spirits and trapped teachers, we have to be worried that the Mutton family will become involved."

George and Maggie nodded sadly. It did seem to George that, slowly but surely, they were getting in way over their heads.

"But now it's more important than ever to be as quick as possible to set everything right. I can't bear the thought of Mum and Dad getting involved," George said feeling a heavy block of dread weighing down his stomach.

Charlie and Maggie agreed but all three couldn't quite believe that they could truly conquer the all-powerful Redwin magic. The time to put Yvonne's spell-work to the test had to be soon.

$$\mathcal{XXX}$$

A plan, George thought to himself as he sat in his bedroom babysitting his two little brothers, *we must have a proper plan to defeat Uncle Hubert.* George had spent the last two days wracking his brain relentlessly trying to form an air-tight plan for himself and his fellow investigators, but to no avail. Now that George realized the extent of Uncle Hubert's wicked ways he was growing more and more apprehensive about how he would go about his next move.

"What do you say, little guys? Any suggestions?" George asked his two baby brothers.

Ben and Bob gurgled in reply, swinging their miniature arms through the air.

"Thought not." George said, putting his head in his hands to once again go over the Regale Mystery.

We have a Redwin capable of magic, but is Yvonne any match for Uncle Hubert's power? A thought had been gnawing at him over the last two days; George was terribly worried for Yvonne. Were they all putting her in danger? *Yes*, George answered himself, *but there's no other option*. George knew that it could only help to get Miss Roland in on their plans and the only way to talk to her safely was to be in an enclosed house so that they weren't overheard. But Miss Roland could not leave her house, due to her ghostly guards haunting her every solitary moment. So they needed Yvonne to use her Redwin magic to dismiss the guards long enough to have a conversation in private with Miss Roland, but then what? The guards would surely tell Uncle Hubert and then Yvonne would be in trouble.

George flung himself onto the bed, burying his face into the pillow. If only Uncle Hubert would order Yvonne to take over summoning the guards for one night. And then it hit him, if Yvonne could gain enough trust from Uncle Hubert and trick him into believing she enjoyed the horrid responsibility of imprisoning Miss Roland then she could order the guards just a bit late and give her friends time to secretly talk to their teacher. The plan was still fraught with danger and so many things could go wrong but it was better than nothing. George carried his brothers from the room, intent on calling Charlie with his new plan and was walking down the hallway to deposit them in their bassinets when Ben let out a sudden shriek.

"What's wrong, little one?" George said soothingly, but then Bob let out an identical shriek.

George looked hard at his baby brothers, trying to figure out what was wrong; then he noticed that they both had their eyes fixed on the wall behind him. George spun around, expecting to see a big spider or some other creepy crawly that was scaring the little babies but instead he discovered that one of the stained glass windows behind him was moving. George let out an involuntary yell but he, just like his brothers, could not seem to look away. Thomas Regale was looking distressed in his glass portrait and was beckoning George with frantic hand gestures. The message was obvious: Thomas wanted another meeting. George hesitated before talking to the portrait and reassuring Thomas that he would visit him. George was not looking forward to sneaking out and risking getting caught by his parents again. But as Thomas seemed so urgent, George dared not decline.

"I'll see you tonight," George whispered to the window and it went back to its usual somber pose at once.

"Now don't you go telling anyone," George whispered to his little brothers, as he resumed his walk down the hallway. "Now you guys are in on it too."

XXX

George waited for his parents to go to sleep, and had a terrible feeling that things were going to go wrong. Butterflies danced their dreadful concert in his stomach, making his heart flutter with their ever-beating wings. *Something's not right*, George thought to himself, not knowing exactly how he knew. But something in his gut told him that tonight was fated to disaster. When George felt confident that his parents were asleep, he sneaked out of his bedroom window but, instead of making his way up to the peak of Mount Dusk, he walked over to his sister's window and tapped as loudly as he dared. Maggie's sleep-lined face appeared at the window, looking around groggily; when she spotted George gesturing frantically for her to come outside, she quickly disappeared from view to put a coat on and then climbed out her window into the cool night air.

"Where are we going, George?" She asked, still looking very sleepy.

"To Charlie's and then to visit the Regale trees; something's not right up there and we're going to find out what it is."

Maggie looked uncomfortable "What if we're caught?"

George felt annoyed. Last time he had gone up the peak on his own his sister had thrown a fit and now she was too scared to go. So he started to walk to Charlie's house in silence and Maggie followed, although she looked a bit sulky.

When they got to Charlie's house, they stood on the front lawn, trying to figure out which window was his.

"I think it's that one," George said, pointing to a window on the second floor. George found a couple of rocks and, with great concentration, proceeded to pelt Charlie's window with them. After a few tense moments, where George was very worried that they had gotten the wrong window, Charlie popped his head out. When he spotted George and Maggie, he backed out of his window and quietly met them on the lawn a few minutes later, wrapped up in a big coat.

"It's not that cold," Maggie commented, laughing at the skinny boy drowning in his clothing.

"What the heck are you guys doing here?" Charlie asked, looking worried.

"The Thomas Regale window spoke to me tonight; he wants us to go see him. I think it's urgent."

Charlie thought for a moment "I think we should bring Yvonne, just in case we need some Redwin magic."

The two other friends agreed and waited on the lawn until Charlie came back with his scared-looking sister.

"I don't like this," Yvonne said quietly. "If we get caught, that's it for all of us."

Charlie quickly explained what had happened and they all started to move towards the peak of Mount Dusk. George still had an uneasy feeling about what they were doing, but he couldn't see a way out. He felt very responsible for the Regales now that he had gotten himself involved in their mystery and he knew he would never be able to sleep if he didn't at least go and check up on them.

When they had made it to the foot of the path leading to the peak, George addressed his friends.

"If anyone wants to back out of this, now's your chance."

They all looked around at each other but nobody backed

out, so quickly they scrambled up the path towards the scary trees. George now knew his way to the Regale trees better than last time and directly led his friends to them with only a couple of wrong turns. There they found Thomas Regale looking anxious. Yvonne gasped when she spotted the bark face and Maggie let out a little moan, but everyone stood their ground, waiting for him to speak.

"Children, we are in even worse peril than we have ever been. Listen carefully!" Thomas started in a rush. "We have been informed by our lovely grandchild and your teacher Patricia Roland that the current Redwin, Hubert, shall be mounting this place a week from now to curse dear Patricia into the ground, as his predecessors did to us. I don't know how you can stop him but, please, children, you must try. It is our only hope."

Everyone stood very still after this speech. They were completely shocked at the news that by this time next week Miss Roland could be trapped in a tree forever.

"How on earth are we meant to do that?" Yvonne finally squealed, terror making her voice sound very high.

Maggie nodded at this and stepped forward to address Thomas. "Sir, it's impossible to think that we might have any power over Mr. Redwin. You're asking us to do something that we just can't do; I mean, really, we're only kids."

Here Thomas looked at Maggie with a deep sadness in his eyes. "Indeed, child, it does sound impossible but I ask you, please, to try. Please. I know I cannot make you, and you must leave this place now, it is not safe, but I beg you to think on it and tomorrow please help us."

Everybody said goodbye to Thomas, then they started their way back down the mountain with heavy hearts. George was horrified at the thought of Miss Roland being cursed as her family was but he could not think of a way to save her.

"Well," George said when they had reached the Mutton's back fence, "I suggest that we all get some sleep so that we can meet tomorrow and try to figure this out."

Everyone nodded silently, each thinking furiously about how they could save Miss Roland. George and Maggie climbed silently back in their windows without detection. When George entered his room he was surprised to see that all of the leaf shapes on his ceiling were glowing. *This must be their way of showing that they need help*, George thought sadly, feeling very sorry for the Regales. He climbed into bed but didn't fall asleep for a long time, plagued by horrible thoughts of sweet teachers doomed forevermore.

CHAPTER 10

The Hall Monitor

Wednesday morning dawned cold and dreary; rain bombarded the windows of George's bedroom as the wind sung its haunting song. George was just pulling on his socks for school when Maggie entered the room quietly, looking very solemn in her black school uniform and with a tense look on her face.

"George...I couldn't sleep all night. Please tell me you have a plan for Miss Roland."

George looked pityingly at his little sister then he forced a brave smile on his face, "Of course, Maggie, don't you worry. Meet me in the school library at lunch time and I'll tell you what it is."

Maggie's face visibly relaxed, then she bounced out of the room, reassured of her big brother's plan. When she left, George put his head in his hands; there was no plan but he didn't want Maggie to know that. Now he had to come up with a way to save Miss Roland before lunch! George berated himself for digging himself into an even deeper mess and, in an anxious mood, made his way to school.

The morning at school was the same as any other. Matty grabbed George in a head-lock and George pulled his back hairs until he let go. Charlie walked into the classroom with Yvonne trailing behind him. George gave her a little smile, suddenly very aware of the way Matty had messed up his hair and wished he had fixed it before Yvonne walked in. *No, you don't...because you don't like her!* George yelled at himself, trying to stop blushing before Charlie noticed. Too late.

"Why do you just turn red all of a sudden? Go see someone about that; it's not normal."

George grunted and busied himself with unpacking his school bag. He dearly wished there was something he could do to stop blushing around Yvonne; he was finding the problem was getting worse rather than better as time went on. Not only that, but his speech mechanisms seemed to fail around her too; he had taken to muttering nonsense like *"Yesmh"* or *"Hmyeah"* every time he tried to answer one of her questions wittily. As he was expecting Miss Roland to walk in, it was a surprise when Mildred the receptionist came in and sat down at the teacher's desk. Thinking that the old woman had finally lost her marbles, George stood up and said, "This is Miss Roland's class."

Mildred snapped her eyes to George "Really? I thought it was Antarctica!"

Matty and Billy laughed until Mildred snapped her attention on them too. "Oh, shut it, you dunder-heads. We're not studying ape humor today."

George hid his giggles, completely forgiving Mildred her rudeness as he watched Matty and Billy trying to figure out what the old woman had just said.

"Now today," Mildred started, sounding as annoyed as ever, "we will be looking at history because it is my favorite subject and you can't stop me."

Here Mildred stopped looking stern and her face relaxed

into a wistful expression. "History is for the smart; it's all to do with truth, dates and perfect documentation, and anyone who befouls my favorite subject shall find themselves in deep trouble. It takes a special person to truly love history."

The wistful expression melted off her face as her eyes quickly scanned the class.

"But I doubt I can expect that from any of you. I have always thought that Patricia is far too lenient with you all and I plan to start fixing her mistakes today."

Yvonne tentatively raised her hand. "Excuse me, Mildred, when is Miss Roland coming back?"

Mildred smirked, showing little yellow stubs for teeth. "Scared already, are we, princess? Well, an adult's business is none of yours. Now all of you open your history books and we'll get started."

There was rustling for a few minutes while everyone pulled out their *The Mysterious Mount Dusk* text books.

"What's this rubbish?" Mildred asked, holding the text book belonging to Yvonne's friend Trinity.

"It's our history book," Trinity said, looking uncertain.

George didn't think she had ever been spoken to in such a rude manner.

"All you learn in history is about the town?"

The class mumbled their assent.

"But what about all the great Kings and Queens? What about wars? None of that took place in Mount Dusk and certainly wouldn't be in this book! This is sacrilege!" Mildred cried, looking scandalized. "It's inconceivable! What on earth could have happened in Mount Dusk that was so tremendous it takes up a whole year of history lessons?"

George and Charlie looked at each other and smiled.

"You, boy!" Mildred addressed Billy. "What have you learnt in history this year?"

Billy looked confused for a moment, then said "Well, some rich family started the town, built this school...err...then they left town with some circus show or something and the town ended up abandoned."

Mildred looked appalled. "That's it? My god, this teacher of yours has a lot to answer for! Why on earth would she just prattle on about Mount Dusk in history? It makes no sense, I tell you! Well, from today, I shall be teaching you real history."

Mildred turned around and wrote her name on the board (Miss Mildred) just as a strange thought occurred to George. He was bursting to put it past Charlie but dared not cross Miss Mildred, as she was the grumpiest person George had ever met. He would have to wait until lunchtime, when he could gather his friends in the library away from the watchful eyes of their new teacher.

XXX

The lunch bell rang and, as quick as he could, George packed up his gear, prodded Charlie in the back to make him hurry up and signaled to Yvonne to follow suit. The three friends hurried up the corridor towards the library, brother and sister looking quizzically at each other. They arrived at the library and found a secluded table at the back of the room. George did not want to be overheard. Maggie joined them a few moments later and everyone sat looking expectantly at George.

"Okay, I have this idea. Do you think the reason Miss Roland only teaches Mount Dusk history is because she wants someone to figure out what's happening to her?"

Nobody spoke as they thought about George's idea.

"Well," Charlie said eventually, "I guess it kind of makes sense, but why wouldn't she just pull one of us aside and tell us; why would she just hint at it subtly every day?"

George had his answer ready. "Because she doesn't want to be an irresponsible adult. The parents would go nuts if they found out she purposefully put students in danger. But if she was to put the idea in our heads, with no encouragement on her behalf, then no one could say she was negligent and it's not her fault if her students can't help themselves."

Everyone seemed pretty agreeable to George's thoughts. The more they thought about it, the more it made sense. Miss Roland would be desperate for help but, because Uncle Hubert made it his business to go about town charming all the adults, no one would believe her plight. Children, on the other hand, Uncle Hubert underestimated and had no time for.

"I think you're right, George," Maggie said, looking proudly at her brother. "But what was that plan you were going to tell me about?"

George was ready for this too. "My plan is an old one, but I've changed it a little bit. Remember we were going to get Yvonne to delay the Redwin Guards' arrival to Miss Roland's house one night so that we'd have time to talk to her? Well, instead of just talking to her...we're going to sneak her out of her house and hide her so that Uncle Hubert can't find her and curse her."

No one looked as if they agreed with George now.

"Oh that's just about the most dangerous plan I've ever heard of; could you possibly put us in a more risky situation?" Yvonne said, rolling her eyes.

"No, think about it!" George butted in quickly, with his stomach squirming after Yvonne's disagreement. "If he can't find her, how can he curse her?"

"Yes, George, it makes sense; we get it," Yvonne continued. "But where are we going to hide her exactly?"

Here George was stumped. He hadn't had enough time to think that far ahead. He had been hoping for his friends to come up with something. He was just about to retort angrily that maybe someone else could think of a better plan when Maggie leaned forward.

"What about our house?"

Even George started to look skeptical at this.

"You don't think Mum will mind our fugitive teacher camping in one of our bedrooms?"

"Well," Maggie continued, looking nervous. "It was her family's house after all and I thought maybe if..."

"Enough!" Yvonne interrupted. "If we decide to hide her, and I'm not saying I agree with that, then it has to be somewhere actually away from this situation, but close enough to allow us time to get her there before the Redwin Guards are suspiciously late. Somewhere Uncle Redwin would never think to look."

"Like your house?" Maggie asked innocently with a sly look in her eye.

Everyone stopped talking and looked at Maggie. It was a crazy idea, an impossible idea. But George had to give it to her—it made the most sense. George was just about to congratulate his little sister when a loud cough behind him nearly made him jump off his chair.

"*AHEM!*"

George turned around and found himself looking at a girl around Maggie's age with a large round head, big round glasses and braces on her teeth.

"Can we help you?" George asked uncertainly.

"Yesh, you can help me," the girl lisped, spraying George with spit. She couldn't talk properly through her braces. "You guysh aren't shupposed to come to a library just to talk! If you not sheeking a book, then get losht!"

George stared in shock at this stern, strange girl.

"You can't tell us to get out," he said indignantly. "Who are you?"

The girl puffed out her chest importantly. "I am Shamantha, the hall monitor and I am in charge of mishconduct everywhere including the library, thish ish not a club houshe; it ish for reading, sho out, before I tell my grandmother who I believe is teaching your classh as of today."

George reluctantly got up with his friends and left the library. He could definitely see how Mildred and Samantha were related.

xxx

The afternoon progressed slowly after lunch. Mildred rambled on about famous Kings and Queens rapturously as the class stifled yawns. When the bell rang for the end of school there was a rush to push outside into the fresh air as far away as possible from their unwelcome new teacher. The skies had stopped dropping rain, although sinister clouds still hung low, threatening to unleash their watery load. George and Maggie were walking home from school, accompanied by Charlie. Yvonne had gone home to keep up the appearance that she still despised them. George thought that Maggie's idea of hiding Miss Roland at the Redwin residence was brilliant. The castle was huge with many rooms for hiding and Uncle Hubert would never think anyone had enough nerve to hide from him in his own house.

There were two major problems concerning the plan, however; the first was that Miss Roland might refuse to hide in her enemies' house and the second was the chance that Uncle Hubert may stumble across the hidden teacher. Here Yvonne offered her help. She had agreed to find out which rooms Uncle Hubert never entered and, when she found that out, then the only problem was Miss Roland's acceptance, which no one could help, so they would just have to hope for the best.

Charlie was to be having dinner with the Muttons tonight and was looking forward to Mrs. Mutton's usual delicious cooking. The friends trooped into the house and all decided to sit in the backyard with a warm cup of hot chocolate and a bowl of potato chips. It was a very nice way to spend the afternoon until dinner time and George couldn't help but feel that Yvonne should be there enjoying it with them. George finally had to admit it to himself; he had a huge crush on Yvonne. But as far as George could see, there was just no way that they could ever go out together. First of all, Yvonne was his friend's sister and a twin at that. Second of all, George had serious doubts that she liked him back. There was that funny look she gave him in class one time, but the more George was with Yvonne the more it meant less to him. Yvonne had no trouble talking to him and being in close proximity to him; George, on the other hand, couldn't stop blushing, couldn't talk properly and was always stealing glances at her pretty face and exceptionally shiny black hair that looked to George as if it was made of silk.

Charlie interrupted George's depressing thoughts with an interesting question.

"Do you think Miss Roland could have left town already? How do we even know she's still here?"

George thought about it. The Redwin Guards only bothered her at nightfall; she could very well have escaped during the day, if Uncle Hubert was unaware of her leave from teaching. The friends decided that they would wait until tomorrow to check out her house; tonight they were going to take a break from mystery and just be normal kids.

CHAPTER 11

Miss Roland

By the weekend, everyone had decided to try Maggie's idea of hiding Miss Roland in the Redwin residence and a plan had been formed for how they would do it. Yvonne was to tell Uncle Hubert that she had followed him one time, knew what he was doing with the Redwin Guards and wanted to give it a go. Then, if she succeeded, she was to delay calling them until George and Charlie safely got Miss Roland out of her house. Maggie would be waiting in Charlie's room with a rope hanging out of the window ready for Miss Roland to climb then once everyone was safe in Charlie's room they all would wait until Uncle Hubert went to bed and hide her in the room Yvonne had found that Uncle Hubert never went in—the cold tower.

"I think Uncle Hubert's afraid of that room," Yvonne had confided in George one morning.

"Oh, ummm, yeah," George had stuttered in reply.

Yvonne gave George a suspicious look and continued.

"When he needed a book from the tower, he stopped at

the foot of the stairs then told me to get it for him. I don't know why he would be, though."

George nodded, blushing as usual.

XXX

Saturday morning was full of anxiety for George. That very night was the attempted rescue of Miss Roland and only today did George realize how risky their plan was. Miss Roland might refuse. The Redwin Guards might notice that Miss Roland wasn't in her house. Uncle Hubert might discover them getting Miss Roland into the castle. George was thinking of these possible problems over and over again while he was eating breakfast, and he was finding it very difficult to swallow.

Maggie had spent the morning checking out Miss Roland's house and confirmed that she was in there. Maggie had seen her check the mail and said that she looked very stressed. George in the meantime paced his room, going over the plan in his head; it seemed to calm his nerves drilling it into his mind. By twelve o'clock, Maggie, Charlie and George were together and decided to chance walking up to the peak of Mount Dusk to warn the Regales of what was happening. Maggie looked frightened about going back up there but kept her head held high as they climbed. Once at the top, they headed straight for the dense clump of Regales and this time Thomas wasn't the only face out. A young girl about fifteen years of age had her face protruding from a tree.

"Hello," she said in her airy voice. "I am Gwyneth Regale, Thomas's daughter."

George thought she looked familiar; then it hit him.

"Hey, you're the oldest girl in the glass windows at my house."

The girl nodded as Thomas spoke.

"My friends, do you bring good news? You should not be here now that Hubert Redwin is visiting us."

99

"How often does he visit you?" George asked.

"Since about a week ago, it's become almost daily. He likes to sit here and tell us the story of how our dear Patricia is so scared; it is awful."

A pang of pity twinged at George's heart.

"Yes it would be," he said quietly. "And yes we do bring good news...well, I hope it turns out to be good news."

Thomas's fear-stricken face relaxed a bit.

"It has been quite a long time since I have heard those words."

"I can imagine," George answered seriously. "We have a plan, a plan to hide Miss Roland—ah—Patricia."

"Thank goodness! What is it?" Thomas asked impatiently.

"Tonight we are going to delay her ghostly guards and hide her in the last place Redwin would look for her...in his own house."

Thomas and Gwyneth both gasped but it was Gwyneth who spoke.

"But that is far too dangerous!"

"No," Thomas said grimly to his daughter. "I agree it is dangerous but the danger she is in now is far worse. Thank you for taking the time and risk to tell us this news. I pray for everyone's safe passage through the night. Now go before you are found out, dear children."

The three friends bid the Regales goodbye then made their way back down the mountain.

"They're still a bit scary, aren't they?" Charlie asked softly.

His two friends agreed but luckily their pity and sense of duty far outweighed their fear, so they were able to brave the scary trees and help.

XXX

The afternoon flew by far too quickly for George's liking. It was now nearing dusk, the time to go to Miss Roland's house and wait for darkness to conceal them and Yvonne.

Maggie was as pale as a ghost as they walked her to the Redwin residence where she was to wait for her friends and Miss Roland. The boys set up the room comfortably for her, put on her favorite movie about horses and told her that they'd tug on the rope hanging out of the window when they arrived. Before they left they checked that the rope was securely tied to Charlie's large and, more importantly, heavy bed. Luckily, the Mutton children had gotten no objections from their parents when they asked them if they could stay at Charlie and Yvonne's house. Indeed, they looked relieved, as they were now so busy with the twin babies.

George and Charlie walked out of the Redwin castle as if they were heading for their deaths. George's heart beat its frantic protest against his ribs and, by the sickly look on Charlie's face, George guessed that his friend felt the same way. Trying to control the panic that welled up inside him, George talked about normal things like school to Charlie but Charlie just shook his head; he was far too nervous to talk. So the boys walked in silence until they came to Miss Roland's secluded property.

"We should hide over there," George whispered, pointing to a clump of bushes just off to the side of the house.

Charlie nodded, his face pinched and pale.

The wait for nightfall was torture. Every rustling of leaves made George's heart pump wildly. Every breath of wind chilled him to the bone, so it was with grim relief that he spotted Yvonne walking quickly toward them, looking around in search of her friends.

"Psst, over here!" George said in as loud a whisper as he dared.

Yvonne walked shakily over to him.

"I only just convinced Uncle Hubert to let me do this, so please hurry up; he might come down to check on me."

George and Charlie gave each other one last miserable look then they jumped over Miss Roland's back fence and let themselves into her back door. Miss Roland's house was very pleas-

ant and, under normal circumstances, George would have enjoyed looking at her lovely furniture that seemed to smell of
apple and cinnamon. George and Charlie stood in the kitchen,
unsure of where to go first, when Miss Roland walked into her
kitchen and gave an almighty scream.

"SHHH!" George and Charlie hissed in unison.

"Boys!" Miss Roland gasped, clutching her chest. "What are
you...oh, it doesn't matter. You must leave. I cannot explain but
it is not safe in this house—"

"We know," George cut in. "That's why we're here. You
need to come with us; we're going to hide you from Hubert and
we only have a few minutes to do it."

Miss Roland looked at the two boys in shock for a moment,
then grimly nodded her head, grabbed her purse and followed
the boys outside into the chilly night air. They passed Yvonne
with a curt nod and, as they half-ran out of sight, they heard
Yvonne call the dread Redwin Guards. The three escapees started to run, their hearts in their mouths until they reached Charlie's window. Miss Roland looked suspiciously at the rope.

"Hurry!" Charlie whispered after tugging the signal to Maggie.

Plucking up her courage, Miss Roland started to climb up
the rope to Charlie's window. After making sure that their be-
loved teacher had at least made it halfway they crept through
the front door and were just about at Charlie's door when a
cold voice echoed off the high ceilings.

"And where have you two been?"

George and Charlie looked around in horror and saw Uncle
Hubert slowly walking towards them from the direction of his
study.

"Let's see," he continued, a dangerous glint in his small,
cold eyes. "Sweaty, dirty and sneaking about. I think I can sum
up what has happened here."

George couldn't breathe. After all of the planning, all of the
precautions, they were caught at the most simple stage of the
rescue.

"You have been following your sister!" Uncle Hubert thundered.

Charlie looked terrified and muttered a high squeak.

"But luckily before I sent her out on an...errand for me I taught her how to fend off unwanted company; bet that gave you two imbeciles a shock."

Uncle Hubert was smirking. He didn't know! He thought that Yvonne had blasted them away from her with Redwin magic! Quickly contorting his expression to look sullen, he answered Uncle Hubert.

"Yeah, what was that? There was all this light and..."

"It does not concern you," Uncle Hubert cut George off coldly. "Just know that if you two are ever nosy again I will be the one punishing you, but I must remember to congratulate Yvonne; you two look hilarious indeed."

And with that, he swept out of sight down the staircase, no doubt to check on Yvonne.

Shaking uncontrollably the two boys entered the bedroom to find Maggie and Miss Roland looking scared stiff, sitting on the edge of the bed.

"We heard Hubert. Does he know?" Miss Roland asked urgently.

"No," George answered, slumping down on an armchair. "He thought we were just playing a prank. He'd never think kids could do something like this, I'm sure."

Everyone looked very relieved for a moment but then Charlie voiced something rather unnerving.

"What if Yvonne doesn't clue on to Uncle Hubert's congratulations and he finds out Yvonne didn't blast us away?"

No one answered this, as everyone was too tense to speak. They all waited in silence for Yvonne's return home. After twenty minutes of dense silence, the occupants of Charlie's room were finally allowed to breathe easy. The front door opened with its usual musical hinges and everyone sat smiling at each other.

"Miss Roland, in here!"

Charlie had opened his large walk-in wardrobe for Miss Roland to hide in. They all heard Yvonne walk past Charlie's door and into her own room, where she would wait for Uncle Hubert to go to sleep before she braved sneaking into Charlie's room.

Maggie left the boys to go and join Yvonne, as Maggie was known by Uncle Hubert to be Yvonne's friend.

"Oh I'm so tired!" Charlie moaned, throwing himself on the bed spread-eagled.

"You're not the only one," George replied, rubbing his itchy eyes. "But we're not done yet; we have to hide Miss Roland comfortably in the tower before we're done."

George walked over to the wardrobe to let Miss Roland out since they couldn't hear Uncle Hubert stomping about anywhere nearby. But when he opened the door, he discovered her rolled up in a ball, asleep.

After over an hour of trying to stay awake, Charlie's bedroom door opened and there was Yvonne smiling triumphantly. Without thinking, George ran over and gave her a hug.

"You were brilliant!" he told her and beamed at her.

And then it hit him. He was hugging Yvonne! George quickly let go, muttering, "S...sorry, ummm, that was really good...yeah."

But Yvonne hardly noticed. She ran over to Charlie, gave him a hug and asked how their half of the mission had gone.

"Really good! Nothing wrong so far, except that run-in with Uncle Hubert."

Yvonne related her side of the terrible ordeal.

"The Redwin Guards were awful!" she told them with a shudder. "They aren't completely see-through, more like faded, floating people than anything. The woman is as evil as they come; I couldn't see her eyes through the mask she wears—it was just all black and horrid. Then there was the man! Half unicycle! When you look close enough, you can see where his upper-half was stitched onto the bike. It was disgusting!"

Everyone felt a bit sick after hearing this and sat to collect their thoughts for a while. Now was the time for the last stage of the plan: hiding Miss Roland. They decided that Charlie should be the one to hide her since if any of the others were caught they'd be in more trouble. Uncle Hubert already expected Charlie to fail him.

The girls woke Miss Roland up as George prepared Charlie for the nerve-wracking ordeal ahead of him.

"Now remember, you run from corner to corner with Miss Roland following you so that if you're caught Uncle Hubert can't see her."

"Got it," Charlie said. "Now, let's go, Miss, before I wimp out."

Miss Roland looked around at the children.

"I just want to say that I thank you all from the bottom of my heart. You have all risked so much for me and I shall never forget it."

Everyone smiled at the lovely teacher then ushered her and Charlie from the room.

George's nervous system was under serious strain. He felt as though he'd just spent a whole week waiting for something terrible to happen. He would be very glad when Charlie was safely back in the room. But that didn't happen for an hour. Knowing that it should have taken about twenty minutes to hide Miss Roland, George was very worried that, after all of their efforts, everything had gone wrong. Yvonne and Maggie were hugging each other on the rug, while George paced the room muttering things like: "Oh come on!" and "This was so stupid." But, eventually, the bedroom door opened and a white-faced Charlie entered the room, clutching his chest.

"Well, that was horrifying!" He exclaimed, sliding down the door onto the floor.

George leapt up and helped his friend walk over to the bed where Charlie slumped down.

"I was halfway to the tower, right? I heard a noise just ahead of me; it was all dark and I had no idea what it was. So I crept up and Rosemary was there dusting a painting!"

"Why on earth was she dusting at eleven o'clock at night in the dark?" George asked, thoroughly confused.

"Well, that's what I was thinking, until I saw that her pockets were bulging and I heard her mutter: 'If you're going to pay me nothing, don't expect any loyalty from me, Sir.'"

George laughed "She's been stealing?"

Charlie joined in the laughter. "I know! Isn't it great? I'm glad she's paying Uncle Hubert back for how he treats her. So I had to wait for her to leave which she did after about ten minutes. I got Miss Roland up to the tower, set up a bed of blankets for her, and was just about to leave when, out of the tower window, I spotted the Redwin Guards on the front lawn."

Everyone gasped, horror-struck.

"I know," Charlie said, seeing their faces. "I was terrified. So I was looking out the window when I saw Uncle Hubert march up to them and shout at them for leaving their posts. Well, the guards can't talk, I don't think, because they just kept shaking their heads, I think they were trying to tell Uncle Hubert that Miss Roland wasn't at her house. But Uncle Hubert wouldn't listen to them. The idiot just sent them right back!"

Yvonne let out a great sigh. "Oh, thank goodness he didn't realize what they were trying to tell him!"

"Yeah," George agreed, thinking of how lucky they'd been tonight.

"So I had to wait until I heard Uncle Hubert go back to bed before I left the tower. I tell you, I nearly peed my pants when I saw those guards."

"I think I was close to it, just hearing about the guards!" George replied and the two boys giggled, while Yvonne rolled her eyes.

"Well," came Maggie's high voice. "We've done it! We actually did it!"

Then it hit them, the sweet victory of it all, and for the rest of the night they celebrated with laughter and blow-by-blow accounts of the adventure until sleep took hold of the exhausted rescuers.

CHAPTER 12

Practice

*T*he weather got warmer in the town of Mount Dusk as summer set in full blast. Days were slower as it was way too hot for any form of fast movement and George preferred to spend these days sitting next to his family's lawn sprinkler. George felt wonderful after the successful rescue of Miss Roland and a week had gone by without her detection by Uncle Hubert. Yvonne was visiting her daily with food and clean clothes and reported that Miss Roland was very happy with the fantastic view she had from the tower and the satisfaction of having escaped Uncle Hubert and the guards.

School without Miss Roland was very irritating. Mildred took up whole days talking about her favorite war facts and stories of witch burnings. She punished anyone who spoke during class with hall duty and, as that involved talking to Samantha the hall monitor, it was severe punishment indeed.

One morning George's pen ran out of ink and, as he was asking Charlie for a lend, Mildred loomed above him.

"Well well well, if it isn't Mr. Chatty," she said quietly, putting her face level with George's. "When the bell rings, you are to report to Samantha for the whole of lunch; let's see if that won't cure you of your naughty ways."

George was furious. He was not looking forward to being spat all over by "Spraying Samantha" as he now called her. The lunch bell rang and Charlie slapped George on the back pityingly as he walked morosely towards the library to meet Samantha.

"Ooo, look who it ish," she spat smugly as George walked over to her. "Sho, decided to tesht my grandmother, did we?"

George didn't say anything but stood beside her, fuming.

"Hey, George," Matty yelled on his way outside. "Love the girlfriend."

George's face burned brilliant red as he stood next to Samantha, who laughed hysterically at George's humiliation.

"That'sh what happensh to rule breakersh," Samantha said and giggled infuriatingly.

George spent the whole lunch cleaning up the school as Samantha saw fit and by the end of lunch was so fed up he stormed away from her without a backward glance.

"That girl!" he vented to Charlie. "Does she never want friends or something?"

Charlie laughed. "Just make sure you have a working pen tomorrow, mate."

As the days went on, the mystery of Mount Dusk slipped slowly from George's mind, which was very preoccupied with ice creams, Yvonne, swimming, Yvonne and Yvonne. George was managing to talk to her without stuttering and he grinned proudly every time he managed to say "hello" or "excuse me" successfully. In fact, George's life was becoming much more normal until a certain Friday he would never forget.

The day started normally enough with his breakfast of eggs and toast and dressing for school. He was just walking out of the house when he noticed a familiar movement that caught his eye. A stained window was moving. This time it wasn't Thomas

Regale beckoning him but Gwyneth Regale. She was waving him over to her.

"Do you want me to come and visit you?" George asked, dreading the answer.

Gwyneth nodded and George resigned himself to the worst. Tonight he would have to go back up to the peak.

"I'll come tonight," he told Gwyneth, trying to keep disappointment out of his voice.

But to his surprise Gwyneth shook her head.

"Sooner?" George asked.

Gwyneth nodded emphatically.

"But I have school!" George cried to the window.

"What was that, dear?" Mrs. Mutton called.

"Nothing!" George cried back, then, lowering his voice, addressed the window. "I have to go to school."

Gwyneth shook her head and George understood; she needed to see him now. George nodded to the window and it returned to normal. George was worried that, if he didn't show up for school, then Mildred would call his parents, so he did the only thing he could think of; he feigned illness. George told his mother that he had a terrible headache.

"Oh dear me!" she cried. "Well, you hop off to bed. I'm sorry to say, dear, that you'll be left alone for a little while later this afternoon; I have a bit of shopping to do."

And with that she bustled away to tend to the twins. George felt relieved; he had a chance to escape the house without her notice in just a few hours.

George spent the next three hours thinking nervously that the Regales might be angry with him for stopping his work on the mystery. He really had not meant to; it was just that with all of the beautiful sunny days it was very hard to remember that any sort of horror would be alive in this bright little town.

"George, I'm leaving now. Remember to keep the doors locked and I'll be back in about an hour."

George didn't answer, hoping that his mother would think

109

that he was asleep. Apparently she did, because he heard the front door shut very quietly.

George jumped up off his bed, ran to the front window, and watched his mother pull out of the driveway. When she was out of sight, George ran out the front door and raced as fast as his legs would take him up to the peak. Puffing and gasping, George reached the Regale trees in record time. Sure enough, Gwyneth's nervous face was poking out of the nearest Regale tree.

"George, thank goodness! We were getting so worried! We haven't heard how your plan with Patricia went and we were starting to fear the worst."

George felt guilt swirl in his stomach region. These poor souls had enough to worry about and here he was leaving them in the dark for a few summer days.

"I'm sorry, Gwyneth," George said sincerely. "I've been...preoccupied."

Gwyneth looked understandingly at George as he went on.

"The plan went well. Miss Rola...I mean, Patricia is safe and sound in the Redwin castle. Hubert Redwin seems to be scared of one of the towers so that's where she is hiding."

George was surprised to see Gwyneth's face turn into a smirk.

"Of course he's scared of that tower. That used to be the room where his ancestors held any Regales they had captured. It is said that my grandfather died in that room and his ghost still haunts it. I don't know if it's true but, if I were a Redwin, I would be scared to go into that room, too. For our dear Patricia, though, it may just be soothing to have one of her family members floating around."

George found it very amusing to hear that Uncle Hubert was actually scared of the Regales.

"I don't mean to be rude, but is that all you wanted? I have to be back home before my mother notices I'm gone."

Gwyneth looked at George sadly. "You've done an excellent job and I shall tell my father all that you have done."

George looked around at Thomas's tree.

"Why doesn't he show his face?"

Gwyneth looked even more stricken.

"He does not believe that it is possible for us to be freed any more. He is...very distressed."

George felt as if he wanted to cry. Guilt churned in his stomach worse than ever.

"Please tell him that there is hope, because I won't give up," George said loudly.

Then he ran at break-neck speed back home, wiping away his tears as he went.

✕✕✕

After that Friday George worked furiously on the mystery, adamant that he would never have reason to feel that guilty ever again. Even Charlie, who wanted to help the Regales very badly, was surprised. At one moment, when George started yelling at anyone near him to "hurry up and think!", Charlie had to sit him down and tell him off for being such a tyrant.

"I'm sorry," George said. "I just don't know what to do next. We've got Miss Roland and now what? We're back to the original problem—setting the Regales free. And I know Yvonne could practice and eventually learn the spell but then Uncle Hubert would be furious and Yvonne's power is no match for his."

"I know," Charlie said, looking forlorn. "So we're just going to have to deal with that after we set them free."

George looked at Charlie in shock. "We can't do it! It's too risky! He'll kill us all. We have to think of a better course of action."

Charlie shook his head. "There isn't one. I'd like to believe that there was a safer way to do this but there's nothing for it; we'll just have to bite the bullet and do it, safe or not."

George felt deflated. So this is what it came down to; an inevitable stand-off with Uncle Hubert. It was a scary thought, an impossible victory, but in his heart of hearts George knew that Charlie was right.

"Well then, let's start training you and Yvonne for the fight of our lives."

XXX

Yvonne proved to be much more capable of Redwin magic than Charlie. On the weekend the four friends met up in the Mutton backyard to practice some Redwin magic while George's parents went for a picnic with the twins. Mrs. Mutton had pleaded for her two eldest children to accompany them but George and Maggie had refused. Time was pressing.

"Oh Charlie, your arm goes up straight! What is that? Your arm's all limp and pathetic," Yvonne yelled at her brother.

"Well, excuse me for getting a little tired after two hours!" Charlie roared back.

He had been getting quite frustrated at himself for not being able to do anything at all to be considered magical.

"Look! Let's stop for a popsicle," George said and disappeared into the cool of the house to fetch some raspberry flavored ice treats.

When he returned, he found his three friends all standing around a flower, looking shocked.

"Oh, what did I miss?" moaned George, who hated to miss out on anything.

"He did it!" Yvonne cried, jumping on her brother. "He made a rose bud bloom!"

George and Maggie cheered as Yvonne and Charlie whirled around happily.

"Now I just have to learn the difficult stuff," Charlie said, bringing everyone back down to earth.

"Oh yeah, that," Maggie said, looking disappointed.

"Oh, come on, Maggie," George scolded. "We all knew why we really wanted Charlie to learn this. Not for fun; for people's lives."

"Yeah, I know," Maggie answered, letting herself drop to the ground dejectedly. "But it's so scary and so awful to think that we have to fight Uncle Hubert face to face."

Everyone sucked on their popsicles reflectively. Maggie looked like she might cry in fear when Charlie plucked the rose he had just made bloom and handed it to her.

"I swear I'll make one bloom just for you every day until this is over."

Maggie smiled at the pretty blossom and, heartened by her change of mood, the friends re-doubled their efforts.

"Golden light!" Charlie cried, pointing to the rosebud.

"What are you trying to do now?" George asked.

"Trying to turn it gold," Charlie answered.

"Golden light!" he cried again, with sweat beads forming on his brow.

And this time one scarlet petal shone brilliant gold.

"Oh, it's beautiful!" Maggie squealed, clutching it to her chest.

"I can do it!" Charlie sang, wiggling his bottom in victory as George and Yvonne laughed.

George was very happy that Charlie was progressing, but couldn't help feeling a little bit apprehensive. Every day Charlie got better was another day closer to fighting Uncle Hubert. George didn't want to show it to his friends but he was absolutely petrified at the thought of it. As soon as Yvonne and Charlie were up to a good standard with their magic they were to set the Regales free and wait for Uncle Hubert to find out. Then, when he did, they would all be fighting for their lives as George had no doubt Uncle Hubert would try to kill them in his anger.

After another hour they were all very tired from their magical efforts and wandered inside for some afternoon tea. George sat next to Charlie and it hit him that he was sitting next to someone who could do magic. It was a very strange thought. When George first met him, Charlie was a timid boy, scared and bullied by everyone. Now he was planning to rid a town of terrible evil with his family magic. It was a huge transformation and George was very proud of his friend.

"What was that for?" Charlie asked, as George gave him a slap on the back.

"You're doing really well, mate; just thought you should know."

Then feeling a bit girly, he added, "But don't think you're too fantastic."

Everyone laughed and George met Yvonne's eyes. For a moment, while their eyes bored into each other's, Yvonne smiled, a gentle smile that made George feel as if his chest was swelling. But as soon as it had started, it ended and Yvonne looked away and began talking to Maggie.

Today's been pretty good, George thought to himself contentedly.

✗✗✗

As the weeks progressed, so did Charlie's ability. He had finished with flowers and now could turn a rock into a plant. Yvonne, of course, could already do this and felt confident that she could reverse the Regale's curse as soon as Charlie was up to scratch. George was just thinking about a particularly great day when Yvonne's long sheet of ebony hair had caught the light just right and seemed to sparkle, when he realized his entire class was staring at him.

"Oh...ah yeah," he said, hoping the answer to whatever Mildred had just asked was "yes."

"The Magna Carta was signed at 'yeah', was it?" Mildred snapped, grating her teeth and looking very agitated.

George didn't actually know what the answer was so he tried his luck at grinning charmingly at the old woman.

"Don't you leer at me, boy!" she cried, wrinkly cheeks wobbling. "I'm old enough to be your granny."

Matty and Billy laughed loudly.

"You're so in, George. Gonna take her for a nice supper at the RSL club?" Billy whispered and Matty laughed again appreciatively.

"Don't worry, I wouldn't want to intrude on your girlfriend there," George whispered back.

Billy looked at him stupidly for a second then turned around, obviously not understanding what George was suggesting. George was getting thoroughly fed up with Mildred's history lessons so, daringly, he raised his hand.

Seeing George's hand waving at her, Mildred grunted for him to speak. "Shouldn't we be learning math or something?" George asked. He never thought he'd see the day where he wanted a math lesson.

Mildred looked momentarily stumped and, taking advantage of this, George continued.

"Weren't you just saying the other day that Miss Roland was wrong in teaching us just the one subject of Mount Dusk?"

Mildred opened her mouth then closed it again; she had no defense.

"Err...well yes, alright. So where are you up to with math?"

"Long division," Trinity yawned.

Mildred paused at the whiteboard with her marker poised to write, then she suddenly walked right out of the classroom. Everyone looked very confused so George followed her to see what was wrong. He found Mildred outside in the hallway leaning up against a wall.

"Miss?" George asked tentatively.

He was shocked when Mildred turned around to reveal tears sliding down her weathered cheeks.

"Miss, what's the matter?"

Mildred shook her head. "I don't know any math."

George was shocked. "Well, no offence, Miss, but why are you teaching then?"

"I used to know math back when I was a teacher at this school. But then my memory started to fail me and they made me the receptionist. I've forgotten everything but my history lessons."

George stared at the bitter old woman for a moment before answering. He would feel sorry for her, but she wasn't a very nice person.

"Perhaps, then, I won't mention math again in exchange for a little something?"

Mildred turned around to glare at him. "Like what?"

"I don't ever want to be put on detention with your granddaughter Samantha again."

Mildred considered this for a while then a terrible smirk spread across her face. "Oh, I won't give you detention with Samantha again, don't you worry, boy."

And with that she waltzed back into the classroom, leaving George out in the hallway to regret ever trying to bribe the awful Miss Mildred.

xxx

The very next day Mildred's punishment for George's attempt at bribery came around.

"George," Mildred called during their reading time. "Follow me, please."

George stood up and followed Mildred out of the classroom.

"Samantha will find you at lunch for detention."

"But...but you said I wouldn't be on detention with Samantha again!" George cried.

"Oh, you won't be in detention with her!" Mildred laughed. "She will be on detention with you!"

George stood there gob-smacked as Mildred laughed at him. A play on words! George asked that he never be put on detention with her again; he never said anything about her being on detention with him.

Feeling as angry as Mildred looked happy, he stomped back

into class, fuming. Charlie gave him a curious look but couldn't talk, lest he face Mildred's wrath.

After a terrible (and very wet) lunch, George returned to class, adamant that he would pay Mildred back. If she was going to get all specific about wording then so would he. George had promised yesterday not to ask her about math again, but he had never promised not to mention any other subjects. As soon as Mildred walked back into class, George's hand shot up into the air.

"What?" Mildred asked, hands on hips.

"What about science?" George asked, meeting the squinty little eyes triumphantly.

But Mildred was ready for him. Slowly she lifted a big science textbook out of her suitcase and smiled. Mildred walked over to where George sat horror-struck; quietly, so that no-one else could hear, she whispered: "I did my homework last night; don't ever try to mess with the master, boy."

CHAPTER 13

A Terrible Slip

At last Charlie had mastered one of the most complicated spells, which involved making someone move against their will. They were at least ready to attempt to free the Regales. But now that they were ready, everyone was very nervous.

"Maybe we should wait," Yvonne said anxiously as the friends sat on George's bed one Saturday night. They were all having a sleep-over at the Mutton residence to prepare.

"Wait for what? There's nothing to wait for now," Charlie said, looking frightened.

"Well," George said, sick of the morose mood, "let's have some ice cream and watch a movie. We don't have to think about the mystery tonight; it's all just making us nervous."

The friends readily agreed and they put on a very funny movie involving a friendly yet clumsy poltergeist. They were halfway through the movie when George heard a knock at the door. Presuming that it was just one of his mother's book club friends, he didn't think about it again.

"Hey, Charlie, come help me fill up these ice cream bowls again."

The boys set off for the fridge, discussing the mystery in hushed voices.

"God, it'll be scary when Uncle Hubert finds out we've freed the Regales. I hope Yvonne and me can beat him when he tries to do us in."

Just as George was about to agree, he heard a noise behind him and reeled around. Standing directly behind them was none other than Uncle Hubert himself, wearing an expression of horrible fury. George felt as if his stomach had just dropped away. Cold terror made his limbs go numb as he gaped at the hulking, evil man. Charlie had started making horrible rasping noises like a mouse out of breath.

"What a nice night for you all," Uncle Hubert said softly; a terrible grin contorted his face. "Pity it will be the last time you see each other. YVONNE!"

Uncle Hubert grabbed Charlie around the neck and dragged him out to the entrance of the house as Yvonne rounded the corner, eyes wide with terror. He grabbed her too, then heaved the two mortified children from the house before turning to address George.

"Tell your parents that urgent family affairs have called us away—if you know what's good for you."

And with that they were gone. George closed the front door, shaking uncontrollably. *This cannot be happening*, he thought to himself wildly. He couldn't believe their terrible luck! Nearly a whole year of planning and this is how it ended.

"No," George moaned desperately, sliding down the wall.

Maggie rushed into the room and spotted George.

"What happened? Where is everyone?" she asked, looking worried.

"Uncle Hubert heard me and Charlie talking. He took them away; it's all over Maggie, all over."

Maggie gasped and covered her mouth.

"What will he do to them?" Maggie asked quietly, her eyes welling up with tears.

"I don't know," George answered, letting his own tears of despair drip down his cheeks.

xxx

It had to have been the worst night of George's life. He had no idea what kind of punishment Uncle Hubert had in store for Charlie and Yvonne, or what he was going to do to him. And, most disappointing of all, they couldn't set the Regales free. George sobbed into his pillow. Why did they have to talk about it out in the kitchen? George was just about to roll over and try to sleep when a soft, urgent knock sounded on his bedroom door. Maggie walked in, her face as white as chalk.

"George, the Redwin Guards, they're here!"

It took a moment for this terrible news to sink in. George was shocked that the situation had managed to get worse. He followed his sister out of the room as quietly as he could while they made their way to the lounge room curtain. And there they were. The woman guard with her elaborate mask and the male guard with his mutilated torso. George fell to the floor, heart pumping wildly. Surely Uncle Hubert wouldn't want Mr. and Mrs. Mutton finding out his true identity, so why did he have these sickening apparitions outside of their house?

"They appeared as soon as Mum and Dad went to bed," Maggie whispered in quivering tones. "I told Mum I just wanted to have a glass of milk before going to bed and as soon as I heard their bedroom door shut, I saw a flash of light through the curtains and there they were."

"So that's his game," George said bitterly. "He knows we can't sneak out while Mum and Dad are awake so when they go to sleep he's got us guarded."

George was suddenly filled with rage. This awful man thought he could terrorize him, did he? With his face burning with anger, George ripped open the front door and shut it behind him.

"Cowards!" he yelled at the guards, who were slowly advancing on him. "You're only scary because you're dead; if you were alive you wouldn't have the guts to fight us, would you?"

Maggie's trembling hands grasped the back of George's nightshirt and pulled him inside.

"It won't do any good, George; we're trapped!"

And after that there was nothing left to do except go to bed and try to rid their minds of Uncle Hubert's punishment.

XXX

George had been expecting to feel like crying the next day, but, to his surprise, he was feeling rather energized.

"This is just another reason," George explained to Maggie as they sat in their backyard, "to work harder."

Maggie shook her head. "But the Redwin magic..."

"We have the Redwin magic!"

"George, you're not thinking straight; we can't rescue Charlie and Yvonne."

"Why?" George cried, standing up and pacing in front of his sister. "Think of all the things we've done. We've faced trees that talk in the middle of the night and those Redwin Guards; we've rescued Miss Roland and we've managed to keep it all a secret for nearly a year."

George sat down next to Maggie and took her hand.

"Please, Maggie, help me."

Maggie paused for a moment. "Oh, I just can't, George," she answered in her little voice. "I'm too scared."

Maggie walked away with her head down and George felt shame come over him. She was only seven and he had expected way too much from her already. *Right, then, it's up to me*, George thought. It was bad enough thinking of Charlie in trouble, but, when he thought of Yvonne, his stomach seemed to freeze inside him. He knew Yvonne was in worse trouble than Charlie, because she had betrayed Uncle Hubert, who had trusted her. Uncle Hubert had never trusted Charlie and so expected nothing better of him. George had never faced a bigger bully than Uncle Hubert in his life and could not just sit around and let him get away with it. First the Regales and now George's very own friends. Enough was enough. And with nothing else to lose, it was hard to restrain himself from storming up to the Redwin castle right then and there and taking his friends back.

XXX

That night George packed his school bag with a torch, some water and a blanket, ready for the morning. He did not have much of a plan but it was better than having none at all. George planned to go to school, feign illness and, when Mildred sent him home, head straight for Charlie and Yvonne. He did not know exactly what he was going to do when he got there but he knew one thing for certain. He had to check if his friends were okay or even still alive.

CHAPTER 14

The Confession

*T*he morning was all gloom and doom with dark skies and screeching wind but George didn't care. All George could think about were his two friends being held prisoner in their own house. On the way to school Maggie was giving him curious looks.

"George, you're not going to try anything stupid, are you?"

George gritted his teeth and shook his head, but the meaning was clear. He was. Maggie was looking very worried and held George's hand until they reached their separate classrooms. George sat down in his usual seat and the sight of Charlie's empty chair stiffened his resolve. He would help his friends escape.

After five minutes of listening to Mildred's never-ending history lesson he raised his hand.

"Oh what?" Mildred snapped, a bit of spit escaping her almost non-existent lips.

"I feel like I'm going to throw up, Miss," George moaned, gripping his stomach dramatically.

"Well, get out, boy! Don't be throwing up near me. I don't care to see what you had for breakfast."

George suppressed a triumphant grin and walked quickly from the school, trying hard to restrain himself from running, in case Mildred saw that he wasn't really sick.

Once George had made it to the footpath outside the school he stopped for a moment to collect his thoughts. When he got to the Redwin residence, he would throw rocks at Charlie's window and hope for the best. George knew that it was a terrible plan but time was of the essence and it was the most he could do. With his heart pumping wildly and the sound of rushing blood assaulting his ears, he walked to the dreaded castle. George stopped a moment at the sweeping front lawn, staring up at the cold grey facade. This was it. Selecting some large round stones from the ground, he proceeded to Charlie's window. His arm was up high ready to swing when a sound caught his attention.

"*Psst!*"

George's eyes swiveled in his head and spotted a bush rustling a few yards behind him.

"Yes?" George whispered, feeling beads of sweat run down his forehead.

"It's us!" George recognized Charlie's voice with a rush of relief. "You'll get us all caught; come over here."

George scrambled over to the bush and ducked behind it. There they were; Miss Roland, Yvonne and Charlie, all grinning at him.

"How did you guys get out?" George whispered, thoroughly relieved that he didn't have to rescue them anymore.

"We'll tell you later," Charlie replied, looking around nervously. "Right now we need to get out and we're going to your house."

"What?" George had a fleeting image of his parents' shocked faces and his mother declaring that they would have to move.

"We don't have a choice, George," came Miss Roland's soft voice. "If your parents agree then we can be safe until we form a plan. Hubert won't want to show them that he's really evil at first."

George accepted this as very true. "Alright, but let's hurry."

The party of four crept one by one off the property with panic hurrying their movements, until they were all clustered at the top of Willow Street.

"Run for it!" Charlie cried, losing his head, and they all ran full pelt to the Mutton residence.

They arrived on the front doorstep gasping for breath after the lengthy run. George was absolutely dreading telling his mother all that had been going on but swallowing his fear, he pushed open the front door. Mrs. Mutton was seated in an armchair singing to Ben and Bob. When she looked up, shock made her eyes wide and round.

"My goodness! What's happened to you all?"

George walked up to his mother and gently laid a hand on hers.

"Better make some tea and sit yourself down, Mum; it's quite a story.

✗✗✗

After the story had been told, Carol Mutton sat looking stunned. A couple of times she opened her mouth as if to speak, then shut it again and shook her head. Finally her eyes met her son's.

"Do you have any idea how much danger you've been in?" Her voice was cold and tight with shock. "Why on earth have you waited so long to tell me?"

George hung his head and stared at his lap.

"I was worried you'd want to move before we got to free the Regales."

Mrs. Mutton opened her mouth angrily but stopped as she saw a tear run down George's flushed cheek.

"Oh, George!" She cried and wrapped her arms around her son. "You've been so brave! And I can hardly believe that Maggie has been helping. Looks like the Mutton children are stronger than their parents gave them credit for."

George looked up in surprise, "You're not angry?"

"Well, yes, I am," Mrs. Mutton started gently. "But I can hardly stay that way after hearing all that you have done in the name of good. I'm absolutely horrified that you've been sneaking out at night, mortified that an evil man and his ghostly friends have been watching you and I just shudder to think what could have happened to you all. But at the end of the day, I must admit that I can understand why you've done this and I'm glad you came to me in the end for help."

George smiled at his mum. "You'll let Miss Roland, Charlie and Yvonne stay then?"

"Oh, heavens, no!" She cried. "That's far too dangerous. And you best believe that you and Maggie are grounded for as long as I legally can ground you. But we won't move house, so don't worry."

George stared open-mouthed at his mother. For one wonderful moment he had believed she would help, forget all of his wrong doings and just help. But no, in the end she was being an over-protective mother. He could have screamed in frustration.

"Mrs. Mutton?" It was Miss Roland speaking tentatively from the corner. "I don't think I have to point out that your children saved my life and my sanity. They have worked tirelessly to help my unfortunate family; do you really think they deserve punishment?"

She had gone too far. Carol Mutton's lips went very thin and her cheeks flushed an angry red. Luckily, before she could answer, the door swung open and Mr. Mutton stood on the threshold, looking confused at the little gathering in his sitting room.

"Carol, dear, I didn't know we were having guests."

"We're not!" Mrs. Mutton said firmly, glaring at Miss Roland.

126

"Because I will not house people who would agree with putting innocent young children in danger."

Miss Roland blushed and looked ashamedly into her lap. Mr. Mutton looked shocked at his wife's harsh words.

"An explanation?" he asked George.

"Okay, Dad," George sighed. "Grab a cup of tea and sit down."

❌❌❌

After two hours of George's dad slapping him on the back and commenting on his first-born son's obvious bravery, a deal was struck.

George's mum gave in reluctantly. "Okay, you may all stay here, but if this isn't all fixed in a fortnight, then you all have to leave our house and I will move my family to a safer town."

Nobody was feeling completely happy with the deal since a fortnight was a short time to fix a problem that had been going on for centuries, but it was better than nothing. Mrs. Mutton had finally been persuaded by the look of delight in her husband's eye.

"Just think, sweetheart," George's dad said enthusiastically, "we could be a part of possibly the greatest story of good versus evil!"

When Maggie walked into the room after school, she let out a shriek of surprise at seeing her previously imprisoned friends and whimpered as she met her mother's withering gaze.

"So, here enters the last renegade investigator."

Maggie went red. "I'm sorry, Mum, but you have to admit it would have been pretty weak if I hadn't tried to help."

"No," Mrs. Mutton said stubbornly, although her eyes softened a notch. "Not weak—sensible. Where on earth did you children pick up the idea that this was alright? I'll never understand it."

Maggie and George looked at each other and grinned; that was their mum, safety first.

The night was filled with chatter as the finer points of the Regale mystery came pouring out. By nine o'clock, Mrs. Mutton had had enough and insisted that everyone go to bed.

"Maybe I'll wake up and all of this will have been a bad dream."

Charlie slept in George's room, Yvonne in Maggie's and Miss Roland rolled out the sofa bed and slept in the lounge room. As George went to get a glass of water before going to bed, he spotted Miss Roland staring out the window.

"He'll know we've gone by now and those guards won't leave us alone."

George went over and looked out of the window as well. The Redwin Guards were drifting around the house.

"They're pretty disgusting, aren't they?" George asked quietly. "Especially the half-bike guy."

Miss Roland nodded slowly.

"Yes, I've been haunted by them for many years and I've never been able to get used to them." Miss Roland looked at George with big, sad blue eyes. "I will never be able to thank you all enough."

George felt a lump in his throat; this poor, gentle woman had suffered so much.

"I'm glad to help," George choked out and, with a swift kiss on the cheek, he left his former teacher to her thoughts. Even if they didn't defeat Uncle Hubert, at least they had stood up for this lovely woman and her honorable family.

CHAPTER 15

The Storm

When Miss Roland set eyes on the stained glass Regale windows, she practically leapt with joy.

"Oh, so this is what they look like! Look! That girl looks just like me!"

She was pointing to the portrait of the eldest blonde girl in the last window-family cluster.

"That's Gwyneth," Maggie said, showing off how much she knew. "We've spoken to her, and she's really nice."

"Yes, Gwyneth is very nice," Miss Roland agreed. "I just never knew what she looked like as a person."

As the girls chatted at the window, Gwyneth lifted her head and smiled at her relative. It felt like a happy family reunion as the teacher, laughing merrily, leaned over to place a kiss on the smooth glass cheek. Mrs. Mutton watched with a grudging smile at the touching scene.

"I knew those windows were odd."

Ben and Bob seemed delighted to have guests and they

wriggled and squealed their approval. Miss Roland proved to be a lovely houseguest. She cleaned endlessly and sang to the babies in a voice as pretty as a tinkling bell. Finally, George's mum had another woman to gossip with and she took full advantage of the situation, making a constant stream of tea to wet her tongue in order to talk more.

"So she told me to use detergent on the carpet! I couldn't believe it; everyone knows that a specific carpet cleaner is needed for a paint stain. Oh, the women in country towns are so funny!"

Although the conversation was very dull, Miss Roland took it in her stride, smiling and nodding at all the right moments.

George's dad kept cornering him, asking for stories to be told over and over again. He was very excited about the whole business and reminded them constantly of how he could be useful.

"You might need some contraption built for you, and, you know, George, I would be the perfect man to go to for that." Or "Brute strength could be useful; I mean, you're clever, George, but look at those teensy little arms of yours. Mine, on the other hand, are much bigger and who knows when they could come in useful."

George found the bombardment of comments both funny and irritating. He wished it could just be him and his friends working to set the Regales free, without having to include klutz carpenters and tongue-clucking mothers. Charlie, on the other hand, reveled in the attention Mr. Mutton paid to him and couldn't help but smile when the smell of Mrs. Mutton's cooking wafted through the house.

"Your family is so cool; I can't believe you get them all to yourself for the rest of your life."

George looked incredulously at his friend. "Are you serious? You like all those old man jokes Dad tells and the fussing Mum does? Drives me round the bend!"

Charlie shook his head. "Never mind, George."

"No, tell me what it is you like; I'd like to know and I'm your best friend so I have to know."

"Well, with your mum, she honestly cares that I like my food, really wants me to enjoy myself. I can't remember anyone wanting that for me since my Mum and Dad."

George caught his breath. Charlie usually never spoke about his parents.

"And your dad is so funny, really nice. I can't help but want to be around that."

"Well, I think after you get over the entertainment value, you'll agree with me that they're lame. Just plainly and simply lame."

XXX

Everyone knew what needed to be done; set the Regales free then face the wrath of Uncle Hubert. But George's parents thought otherwise.

"There has to be a better plan than that," Mrs. Mutton insisted. "Either you find a safer way to help the Regales or I will have to relocate my family in order to protect them."

"Quite right," Mr. Mutton agreed readily. "A touch of stealth is needed here. I reckon we should plan a decoy. We'll dress some people up like the kids and, while they're being chased, we'll all leave town."

George put his head in his hands which muffled his next words. "Dad, that's great but what will happen to the poor people being the decoys? They'll be killed and Uncle Hubert will still be at large able to hurt whoever he wants."

"Oh, yeah."

Maggie skipped into the room. "I have a plan."

Mrs. Mutton giggled. "Oh dear, just go play with your teddies like a good little girl."

"My plan is to set ourselves up in hiding throughout the town and close in on Uncle Hubert from all sides to ambush him."

Mrs. Mutton stopped doing the dishes and turned slowly to face Maggie.

"How on earth did you—"

"I made it up last night. On my first week in Mount Dusk I did nothing but explore the town because I had no friends. I noticed that the town is shaped rather like a circle, absolutely perfect for an ambush attack."

George got off his chair and hugged his sister. "You're brilliant!"

"Thanks," Maggie said and walked away grinning with pride.

"Quite a little pocket rocket we have on our hands," George's dad said, smiling at his wife, who looked mortified at her daughter's sinister grasp of attack.

"I always thought she'd be so quiet and sweet..."

And so Maggie's plan went ahead. Everyone was seated around the dining table looking at a large, blank piece of paper.

"Right," George started, drawing a circle on the paper and pointing to it. "This is the town. I think we should pick who goes where now—and why. Any suggestions?"

George's dad threw his arm in the air like a schoolboy dying to give a right answer.

George sighed. "Yes, Dad?"

"Well," he started excitedly, rubbing his hands together. "I think the formation should be big, small, big, small. For instance, kid, adult, kid adult."

"Why?" Yvonne asked, looking confused.

"Well...just sounds like a good pattern."

Suppressing the urge to roll his eyes, George continued.

"I have an idea. Since it's us kids who have to set the Regales free, and Uncle Hubert knows that, the adults should be waiting around the peak of Mount Dusk ready to attack because it will take Uncle Hubert by surprise; he'll be expecting us kids to be there. In the meantime, we kids will come up behind him and hit him with some Redwin magic."

Everyone thought for a moment.

"That's stupid." Yvonne was staring at George and George felt his heart do a little flip-flop of disappointment that she didn't like his idea.

"Why?" he asked, trying to keep the whiney tone out of his voice.

"Because we're assuming that Uncle Hubert doesn't have a plan of his own and we're forgetting about the Redwin Guards."

Everyone nodded and looked impressed.

"Well, what's your idea then?" George asked, unable to keep the sulky tones from the question.

"I think we should wait for him in the school. It's got heaps of rooms to hide in, lots of passageways to run from him and was built by the Regales."

"That's a pretty good plan," Charlie agreed.

"Well done, my dear," George's dad said to Yvonne, messing her hair.

Yvonne yanked her head away from Mr. Mutton with a scowl.

"So, we aren't doing my ambush idea?" Maggie asked, looking disappointed.

"We'll still use it, but on a smaller scale, I think," Miss Roland chimed in. "We should all surround the school and enter through different entrances. Then, when he comes in, we'll all ambush him."

Maggie smiled. "Yes! A great idea!"

"Well," Mrs. Mutton said, "since I won't be there, because I have to look after Ben and Bob, I'm going to go to bed. I don't particularly like hearing my family's plan to get themselves injured."

"Carol dear—" Mr. Mutton started looking sympathetically at his wife, but Mrs. Mutton just bustled away.

xxx

It was all planned. The group had organized their places for the ambush and all that was left was to wait a week for school holidays to start. Mrs. Mutton had point-blank refused to give George and Maggie time off from school. Charlie and Yvonne didn't have to go since they were at great risk from Uncle Hubert. George dragged himself to school, fidgeting in his classes. It seemed pointless to be learning about previous wars when he would be soon participating in one of his own.

"Hey, George, where's your girlfriend?" Matty asked one day, pointing to Charlie's vacant chair.

"Why do you ask? Miss him?" George retorted.

"What?" Matty looked confused but Billy seemed to clue on to what was going on.

"Shove it, George."

George grinned; it was one of the most entertaining things to do: baiting imbecilic bullies.

"Seriously though, where are Charlie and Yvonne?" It was Trinity.

"I think they're sick," George said evasively, hoping that he didn't look like he was lying.

"No they're not. I went to their house and the maid was crying, begging me to tell her where the children were."

George frowned. Poor Rosemary had basically raised Charlie and Yvonne. She would be terribly worried and possibly in danger from Uncle Hubert; George hadn't thought of that before.

"Well, I don't know."

Trinity looked at George untrustingly but stopped asking questions.

At lunch Maggie and George would wander around the school inspecting the hiding places that had been allocated to them for the dreaded night of confrontation. Maggie had been fairly cheery at the prospect of ridding the town of Uncle Hubert, which George found odd; he thought she'd be really scared.

"So how come you're not afraid of being involved in the

Regale mystery anymore?" he asked, munching on a salami and cheese sandwich.

"Well, now that Miss Roland and Dad are going to help, I feel a bit better."

George smiled at his sister. Sometimes he forgot that she was just a little girl. Of course she would feel better with adults involved. George had just taken another bite of his sandwich when a noise behind him almost made him choke. It was the noise of whooshing air, only more high pitched. The Redwin Guards were there, at the school, hiding behind some shrubs. The sight was terrifying. The guards were drifting together, becoming one horrendous apparition in their fight for space behind the shrubs. Maggie's face became deathly pale and, without a word, she got up and ran for the school. George stood for a second longer looking at his transparent stalkers. So now they were watching them in the daytime. The female guard had her head tilted to the side, as if considering George; the male was rocking on his unicycle, as if impatient to get his hands on him. It suddenly struck George that the guards would have been warned not to approach the children when people were around. Feeling brave with anger and shock; George took a step closer to the guards, then another. George kept on inching forward until he was only a couple of meters away. He could see where the unicycle had been roughly attached to the Redwin Guard's body and the flowing black skirts that hung a few inches off the ground with its ghostly wearer.

"You won't win," George said, voice trembling. "I won't let you."

The guards stopped moving. The female guard reached out her hands, as if to choke George, then held her own throat, opening and closing her mouth. The message was clear; she would steal George's voice so she could talk. She started to smile at the look of disgust on George's face. *So that's how they came to be; they must steal bits of people's lives when they murder them.* And they had yet to steal voices. With this sickening thought churning his stomach George made his way back up to the school, imagining what the guards' touch would feel like as they stole your life.

✗✗✗

Since they couldn't visit the Regales, George told the window Thomas Regale about the big plan. Thomas couldn't speak through the glass but his eyes said it all; the look of gratitude was enough. There was one day to go until they faced Uncle Hubert and tensions were running high. Yvonne was ready to hold off the Redwin Guards with her magic until they were all safely in their places at Mount Dusk Academy, and everyone else was grimly determined to see everything through. The only problem that was yet to be solved was Mrs. Mutton, who was so frightened for her family that she would break down into tears without warning.

The night was dark and cool and Charlie was as nervous as could be.

"Look, Charlie," George said calmly, trying to convince his friend that it would be alright, "just imagine what it will feel like to finally be free from Uncle Hubert."

"If we end up free. Keep in mind that my family has been getting away with this for hundreds of years."

"But we have everything good on our side! Have some faith, Charlie, I don't believe for a second that the bad guy will win."

George didn't actually believe this one hundred percent but he wanted to look confident for his friend's sake. Charlie looked a little better and fell asleep long before George, who couldn't stop running through the plan in his mind. Terror coursed through George's thin body every time he pictured himself staring into the cold eyes of Uncle Hubert. George could just picture the anger in them and shuddered that such evil could exist in the world. But there was nothing for it; what had to be done had to be done. George just hoped that, when tomorrow night came, he would still have enough guts to face the haunting figures of the Redwin Guards and the hulking figure of Uncle Hubert.

𝓧𝓧𝓧

Three o'clock in the afternoon and no-one could talk. Maggie sat on an armchair rocking back and forth, muttering comforting thoughts under her breath. Yvonne sat outside, staring into the distance. Charlie was pacing in the hallway with a creased brow and George sat in his room staring out of the window towards the peak of Mount Dusk. There were three hours of daylight left and then Yvonne would say the magic words to hold off the Redwin Guards. Mrs. Mutton had refused to see them all day. She had locked herself in her room that morning after kissing her family and making them promise to stay safe.

Four o'clock, five o'clock, five thirty...everyone was in the lounge room, pale-faced and shaking. Maggie had bitten her lips so badly that a tiny droplet of blood shimmered on her lip.

"I'm very proud of you, Maggie," Mr. Mutton said, quietly hugging his daughter. "I can't believe I'm letting you do this."

"I have to, Dad," Maggie said in a quavering voice. "I helped start this and I'm going to finish it."

Mr. Mutton nodded but looked concerned nonetheless. He had insisted that Maggie's entry spot into the school be next to his so that he could hear her if she needed help.

"It's two minutes to six. I'll cast the spell."

Yvonne stood at the front door and took a deep breath, then she flung it open and, pointing to the Redwin Guards, she screamed, "RELEASE WATCH!"

The guards were taken by surprise and disappeared instantly.

"RUN!" George shouted and everyone started sprinting full pelt towards the peak of Mount Dusk. They weren't sure how long Yvonne's spell could hold off the guards, so they had to act as quickly as possible. George's feet pounded the steep path uphill relentlessly. It was all very surreal; soon the Regales would be free and then they would make their way to the school to confront Uncle Hubert. Everyone was positive that, when the Redwin Guards reappeared, they would inform Uncle Hubert that something was wrong and he would go looking for his enemies. George stole a quick glance behind him and what he saw strengthened him. Five friends with determined faces rocketing along behind him. He was not alone.

They all reached the now familiar trees on the peak of Mount Dusk with hearts racing and energy coursing through their bodies, making everyone jittery.

"THIS WAY!" George bellowed, fighting his way through the dense bushes towards the Regale trees.

The group arrived loudly and Thomas Regale's bark face looked alarmed. "My children! What has happened?"

"We don't have much time, Thomas," George replied breathlessly. Behind him, Mr. Mutton was gaping open-mouthed at the spectacle of a tree talking. "We've come to set you free and then we'll be facing Hubert Redwin."

"No!" Thomas cried passionately. "It will be all of you who replace us in the trees!"

"You don't have a choice, Thomas; we're setting you free and that's it."

Thomas Regale's face was caught between desperate hope and grave concern.

"Thank you," he muttered finally.

Yvonne stepped shakily forward. "Charlie, hold my hand; I need help for this."

"But I'm terrible at spell work!" Charlie said, alarmed that his sister expected him to help.

"JUST DO IT!" Yvonne screamed at her brother and he obediently stepped forward and grasped his sister's hand.

"You know the spell." Yvonne's voice had become gentle as she spoke to her brother. "Say it with me."

138

Taking a deep breath they recited together:

"They of cursed place,
They of dire need,
Be set free as meets our will,
On three they shall be freed,
One for absolution,
Two for the certainty of good,
Three for the spell's release,
And so our will be done!"

Everyone stood silent, holding their breath. It seemed the spell hadn't worked until, slowly, an almighty wind began to whip their faces and, with a massive, ear-splitting groan, five shadows slipped from the Regale trees and slowly drifted upward.

"Thank you, my children. Beware the hand of Redwin!" Was all they heard before the shadows disappeared, leaving behind the biggest windstorm that George had ever seen.

The Regales were free and George could hardly believe it.

A thrill of terror ran up his spine as reality came crashing down upon him again. Uncle Hubert would soon be looking for them to get revenge. George caught his fellow rescuers' attention by waving frantically, as he couldn't be heard over the howling wind. He gestured for them to follow him as he raced as fast as he could back down Mount Dusk towards his school.

As they neared the school and George's legs began to seize up from all of the running, he suddenly heard a high-pitched yell of pain over the wind. Looking back, George saw that Maggie had fallen and was clutching tearfully at her ankle. Just as George and Mr. Mutton went to help her up, a sudden chill made the hairs on the back of George's neck stand up on end. There they were, the Redwin Guards, zooming towards Maggie with hands outstretched.

George went cold with horror as he watched the dread beings close in on his sister.

"MAGGIE!" George screamed and ran for his sister. He

grabbed her under the arm and ripped her off the ground as Mr. Mutton bent to carry her.

"RUN!" Mr. Mutton screamed, eyes bright with fear.

George's breath was starting to burn his side and he desperately massaged it. He couldn't let himself slow down. The memory of the female guard clutching at her voiceless throat spurred him on, and then, they were gone.

"They've gone to get Uncle Hubert!" Charlie shouted at George, who had stopped running to catch his breath. "Run, George! Get to your entrance and then you can rest...until he gets here, anyway."

George nodded and made his painful way to his allocated entrance. After all of the excitement of freeing the Regales and running from the guards he was extremely tired and a terrible thought shot through his mind before he could stop it. *What if I'm too tired to fight?* George's mouth went dry with terror at the thought and with a huge effort he pushed it from his mind. After months of being involved with the Regale mystery, it all came down to this one night with Uncle Hubert. *How could just one man cause so much misery?* George reflected as he crept along the lawns towards the great bulk that was his school. *Well, if one man can cause all of this fear, hopefully six people can erase it all.* The thought calmed him.

"Good luck!" George called quietly to his friends as they separated and made their way alone to different entrances.

The plan for defeating Uncle Hubert was in no way a safe one. Basically, it was confront him and take it as it comes. George leaped up a few stairs to get to a partially hidden entrance to the school. On his first week at Mount Dusk Academy he had stumbled upon it, while trying to escape Mildred's lashing tongue because he had been late that day. George sat down on the steps, shaking with trepidation. Waiting for the coming confrontation was worse that running from the guards; he had no idea what Uncle Hubert would do to them, or how he would approach them and it was not knowing that made

140

George's stomach turn with fear. And then a movement caught his eye. In the light of the full moon George could just make out a black shape slowly making its way towards him. His breath caught in his throat as the moonlight hit the black figure in the face. It was Uncle Hubert.

CHAPTER 16

The Fight

George scrambled quietly up to the shadows at the top of the stairs and watched Uncle Hubert's slow arrival. He was walking slowly, confidently, and when the moonlight was right, George could see a small smile playing on his lips. And then, just to make the scene more horrifying, came the Redwin Guards, whooshing up the lawn behind their master. While Uncle Hubert's smile was small, the guards' smiles contorted their whole faces; the effect made George's stomach turn. And then, to George's disgust, he noticed that the guards were not just drifting at all but doing a demented dance of merriment at the prospect of acquiring a new voice and other forms of being. Watching the sickly procession, George was filled with a deep sense of hatred for the evil it represented. Filled with renewed determination, George silently slipped into the back of the school foyer.

The air inside the school was still and thick with expectancy. George tried to slow down his heart and breathing, sure that they were so loud it would give him away. In the seconds before Uncle Hubert was due to enter the school, George tried to picture where all of his friends were hiding. Maggie and Mr. Mutton would be behind him somewhere, Miss Roland would be hiding directly across from him at the front desk, Charlie would be crouched next to the front door while Yvonne would be at the very back of the foyer facing the front doors. Just as George's vision was adjusting to the gloom, the front doors were flung open and moonlight bathed the room. Uncle Hubert strode through the doors, the Redwin Guards drifting around him in circles.

"Come out, come out wherever you are..." The cold voice of Uncle Hubert echoed softly off the high ceiling.

"You can't hide for long," he continued mockingly. "My dear friends here will smell you. I believe they gained their sense of smell off a Regale they disposed of—how very fitting."

Drawing upon every ounce of nerve he possessed, George stepped boldly out of the shadows and glared at his friends' uncle.

"Ah, young George," he said, smiling his chilling smile. "To what do I owe the pleasure? I have been wondering why the guards here are so agitated. You may have noticed that they don't yet have voices to communicate, but that will all change soon."

George took a deep breath, willing his legs to stop shaking.

"They're agitated because we have beaten you," George said, surprising himself with his daring.

Uncle Hubert looked politely confused. "Beaten me? I beg to differ, dear boy; I am still here."

"You are, but the Regales are not."

The smile lingered on Uncle Hubert's face for a second as the news slowly sunk in.

"That's right," George continued, trying his hardest to sound clear and confident. "They're gone, we set them free; I suppose your family should have thought twice before trusting

143

you with the job of keeping them cursed, because you failed miserably."

Uncle Hubert's face was a sea of rage. A vein bulged dangerously on his forehead and his nostrils were flared in his terrible anger. George started to feel scared. *What next?*

"You did what?" Uncle Hubert, breathing heavily, just managed to choke out.

"We set them free; they're gone." Charlie had stepped out of his place behind his uncle who swung around to face him.

"Ah, the family failure."

"That's rich, coming from you," Charlie retorted.

George was shocked to see Charlie's face so suffused with anger. But, after his horrendous childhood with Uncle Hubert, George supposed that he shouldn't be surprised at all. Uncle Hubert started looking around him.

"So, how many others have rallied to your cause?"

"Lots," Maggie's high-pitched voice came from the shadows and echoed through the room.

"More than you think," Mr. Mutton said from his hiding place, making his voice lower than usual.

And then someone else came out of hiding. Yvonne.

"Hello, Uncle," she said in a voice as cold as the wind blowing outside.

"Ah, and now it is the family traitor's turn."

Uncle Hubert turned to glare at his niece just as Yvonne lifted her hand to cast a spell. But quick as a flash, a large shape rushed at Yvonne and knocked her flat on her back.

"Mildred!" Yvonne cried in shock, staring at her attacker's face.

"Ah," Uncle Hubert said quietly. "Dear Mildred', thank you so much for joining us. As you can see, the children are causing quite a stir. Keep Yvonne where she is and we'll teach the little scamp some manners, shall we?"

"Of course, my love," Mildred rasped, breathing heavily with excitement, as she pinned Yvonne to the ground.

144

Yvonne's face paled as she struggled against her captor.

"You wouldn't dare touch me!" she shrieked, trying to sound brave.

"Oh yes, I would!" Uncle Hubert thundered back. "You are a black mark against the noble name of Redwin as is your stupid brother here. Guards! Hold him."

The female guard drifted over to a petrified Charlie and wrapped her arms around him, mouth stretched into a grotesque smile.

"Get her off!" Charlie yelled in a high voice.

Sweat was pouring down his face as he struggled with his ancient ancestor.

"I hear that the guard's touch is almost impossible to bear," Uncle Hubert said, smiling at Charlie. "Boiling hot and burns the skin. A fit punishment."

George wanted desperately to help his friend but was too afraid of moving, in case the other guard was called to trap him. Just then a movement caught George's eye. A flash of white zoomed past the scene and tried to escape out of the front doors. Uncle Hubert stuck out his foot and there, sprawled on the floor, was Samantha the hall monitor.

"What are you doing here?" Uncle Hubert yelled at her. "Mildred! You were not meant to bring your granddaughter; what is the meaning of this?"

Mildred dragged Yvonne with her as she switched on the lights and stared in horror at Samantha.

"Why did you come, you foolish girl? I told you to stay put!"

"You told me you were going to get shome groceries, not break the rulesh!" Samantha spat out, looking very confused and scared.

"You and your stupid rules! Some rules have to be broken, girl!" Mildred yelled harshly but her eyes betrayed how scared she was for her granddaughter.

"Why are you shiding with the bad guy?" Samantha asked.

George pitied the poor girl whose only guardian had just shown herself to be on the side of evil.

"Because...Hubert and I are in love!" Mildred declared, looking rapturously at Uncle Hubert.

Uncle Hubert smiled back, but George didn't miss the fleeting look of disgust that crossed his face beforehand. He was using Mildred.

"Mildred, he doesn't really love you!" George yelled at his teacher. "Please believe me. If he can't treat his own niece and nephew nicely, what makes you think he'll treat you any better?"

Hearing this, Mildred puffed up like a bull frog and glared at George. "How dare—" but Mildred didn't get a chance to finish the sentence.

Using the moment of distraction, Yvonne had wrenched herself free and was running at top speed across the room toward the guards.

"STOP HER!" Uncle Hubert screamed, realizing a moment too late what his niece was about to do.

Pointing her hand at the female guard, she bellowed, "Ancestor, be gone!"

Everyone stopped moving, watching the female guard as if in a trance. A high-pitched sucking noise filled the school foyer as the guard let go of Charlie and started spinning around in circles. Very slowly, she was disappearing from the feet up. The woman was grasping at the air around her in a desperate fight to stay where she was. She frantically clawed at nothing and, in the process, knocked off her golden mask. Yvonne screamed and Samantha slumped to the floor in a dead faint. Where the woman's eyes should have been were empty sockets sunk deep into the back of her head, staring blankly at all around her; her nose was just a large slit in the middle of her face. Her mouth opened in a silent scream as she spun even faster. And then, it was over; the sucking noise stopped and she was gone. Uncle Hubert's face was a mask of horror and fury as he turned on Yvonne, eyes alive with hatred.

"GET HER!" he screamed and, this time, the male guard zoomed up to Yvonne, arms outstretched.

"NO YOU WON'T!" Charlie had gotten up off the floor and was now pointing at the male guard.

"Ha!" Uncle Hubert barked. "And what do you think you're going to do about it? You're too weak to be capable of Redwin magic."

"DON'T CALL ME WEAK!" Charlie screamed and looked back to the guard now holding his struggling sister. "Ancestor, be gone!"

Nothing happened and Uncle Hubert started laughing his cold, cruel laugh.

"You see boy? WEAK!"

"Charlie, you have to visualize it happening as you say it; you can do it!" Yvonne's voice was desperate and the pain in her voice was hard to hear.

Wrinkling his brow in concentration, Charlie once again raised his arm. "Mildred! Grab him just in case!" Uncle Hubert cried, a satisfying note of worry in his voice.

But it was too late. Taking a deep breath, Charlie screamed, "ANCESTOR, BE GONE!"

He had done it. The sucking sound returned and Uncle Hubert watched in horror as the male guard started to spin. He too started clawing all around him. He struggled so hard that his badly attached unicycle broke free of his torso, leaving a stump of a body to spin around. For a moment George caught the guard's eye and shuddered at the look of pure terror on his face. He supposed that even the evil could feel true fear.

"NOOO!" Uncle Hubert screamed, as the last of the guards disappeared.

He stood frozen on the spot and then slowly lifted his head. "If it's Redwin magic you want, then its Redwin magic you'll get!" He screamed, hysterical now, and looking straight at George.

But before he could say another word, Miss Roland came pelting out of her hiding spot and jumped in front of George.

147

"I'm the one you want...please don't hurt the children!" she pleaded.

Smiling wickedly, Uncle Hubert raised his hand.

"Ah, the last Regale; I shall have some fun with you. I have a lovely willow tree in my backyard with your name on it."

Charlie and Yvonne both pointed their hands at Uncle Hubert while Charlie spoke.

"You won't get a chance to destroy her, or we'll get rid of you too!"

Uncle Hubert seemed to realize that he was indeed alone and had rivals to his magic. George was just starting to believe that it was going to be over soon, when Uncle Hubert suddenly picked up Miss Roland and bolted towards the staircase to the first floor. Charlie raised his arm at Uncle Hubert and Mildred who had started running after him when Samantha jumped in front of her grandmother.

"Please don't hurt her...she's all I have left."

Charlie's moment of hesitation was enough for Uncle Hubert to get away, but Mildred stopped dead in her tracks half-way up and looked back at Samantha.

"I'm sorry, Samantha; you weren't ever meant to find out. I know how much you love the rules and hate to see me do this, but I swear that you were never meant to know."

Samantha looked bitterly upon Mildred. "But now that I do know, I can never look at you the shame way again, and wonsh more I'm all alone."

And with that, Samantha ran from the building. Mildred paused for a moment on the stairs and looked about to follow Uncle Hubert up, when she suddenly turned and chased after her granddaughter.

"At least she has some good in her, after all," Mr. Mutton said sadly, stepping out from his hiding place, followed by Maggie. "What do we do now? He has Miss Roland, so we had better be careful."

George stood with panic rising fast. How was he going to

save Miss Roland? He thought of his sweet teacher, the last living member of her family, being held by the very person who had terrorized her for so long. The thought of Miss Roland and Uncle Hubert struggling upstairs made something awaken in George—a hatred so powerful that it almost knocked him over. This one man thought that he could walk all over everyone, terrify them, threaten them and have them do his bidding whenever he pleased. The thought infuriated him and a flush of deep anger spread crimson across his cheeks.

"You alright, George?" Yvonne said with surprising tenderness.

The touch of her soft hand on his arm woke him from his reverie. For the good of everyone, he knew what he had to do and would not let himself chicken out.

Before anyone could object, George raced up the stairs.

"George, no!" Maggie and Mr. Mutton cried in unison.

But it was too late.

With his heart in his mouth, George reached the dark landing of the first floor and looked wildly about in the gloom. No one was on the landing and George guessed that they must be in one of the classrooms. As quietly and as calmly as he could, George started to peek into each classroom, barely daring to breathe. After five classrooms, George was starting to get desperate; the huge school had so many good hiding places and he was terrified at the thought of finding his dear teacher too late.

And then he saw them. They were in the sixth classroom. Uncle Hubert had his hand pointed at Miss Roland, who was backed up against a wall. When he spotted George lurking in the doorway, he pointed his free hand at him.

"Neither of you move or I will kill you. I have known the death spell for many years but have never had a chance to put it into practice. I would love to try it on one of you so do as I say."

George swallowed thickly, realizing that he was in great danger.

"Take a seat, George. Before your teacher is cursed, I want

somebody to bear witness to what I have to say. I want some-one to know that I am not just an evil person who goes out of his way to cause harm. I have a very good reason for my behav-ior towards dear Patricia here. SIT DOWN!"

George made his shaky way over to an empty chair next to Miss Roland. The teacher was frozen with fright and seemed unable to tear her eyes away from Uncle Hubert.

"George, do you know why my family cursed the Regales?"

"Because your family was pure evil!" George cried passion-ately. He would not let this man make him beg or pretend to agree with him.

"No, you are very wrong, George," Uncle Hubert said softly. "It all started many centuries ago. The Redwin family was fa-mous back then; they owned a very successful circus and the town of Mount Dusk loved it. They marveled at the woman who could see and smell with no eyes or nose. They flocked to see the man who was half unicycle and still alive. Yes, my family was very popular indeed...until the Regales came to town." Uncle Hubert's voice was bitter as he spoke the name *Regale*.

"The Regales swept in with their fortune, built the school, and the town hall; people deeply respected them. They thought the Regales were very honorable and when Thomas Regale start-ed saying that the Redwin circus was nothing but a freak show made possible by black magic the whole town believed him." Un-cle Hubert paused, eyes unfocused, lost in his own story.

"Not only did everyone stop coming to the Redwin circus, they drove them out of town believing them evil. And all be-cause of the Regale family. My family's fortune was lost, their reputation shattered and their name struck from all records, as people no longer saw them as human, just freaks. But my family had their revenge." Uncle Hubert smiled at his small audience. "Do you see, George? It was the Regales! They ruined my fami-ly; we Redwins had every right to punish them!"

George shook his head sadly. "It was so long ago, why can't you just forget it?"

"NEVER!" Uncle Hubert thundered. "My family would have been poor if we hadn't cursed the Regales and stolen their fortune. People would have remembered my family as freaks! Me included! No, I will never let it go."

George was just about to reply, when the creaking of a floorboard outside stopped him. Chancing a glance at the door, George saw two silhouettes: Charlie and Yvonne. Luckily, Uncle Hubert hadn't noticed as he had gotten carried away with his story. *Keep him talking*, George thought to himself, trying desperately to think of something to say.

"Well, maybe the Regales did hurt your family," George said, trying to sound understanding. "But Miss Roland had nothing to do with it; why punish her?"

"As long as she's free to walk this earth," Uncle Hubert answered slowly, "then the name of Redwin will always be tainted in at least one person's mind and that's...well...not fair. She must go, and with her, the memory of my family's failure."

Uncle Hubert turned around to face Miss Roland who was still frozen with fear. His face was a mask of bitterness as he stared at the last remaining Regale.

Uncle Hubert raised his hand.

"Regale, be go—"

But before he could finish his sentence, a dark shape raced across the room and tackled him.

"I have his hair!" Came Charlie's triumphant voice as Yvonne dashed into the room behind him, carrying the indoor plant that lived in the school foyer.

"George, Miss Roland, HOLD HIM!"

George raced across the room to help Charlie pin his giant uncle down but Miss Roland just stood gaping in terror at the scene.

"Give me the hair!" Yvonne shrieked eyes wide with panic. "And get some skin!"

George dug his fingernails into Uncle Hubert's arm and scraped some skin off.

"Here!" he yelled, thrusting the minute shavings into Yvonne's clammy hand. At that moment, Mr. Mutton and Maggie burst into the room. Mr. Mutton ran to help his son pin down Uncle Hubert and Maggie ran to Miss Roland, guided her to a chair, and tried to pull her out of her terrified trance.

Yvonne tossed the hair and skin with the soil in the potted plant.

"HE OF OBJECT, HE OF ENEMY, MAY YOU BE CAST WHERE MY DESIRES LIE!" she bellowed, frantically trying to finish the spell before Uncle Hubert burst free.

All around the room, chairs and desks were shattering as Uncle Hubert flailed his arms, trying to curse everyone in sight.

Yvonne ripped a leaf off the plant and tossed it in the soil.

"I CURSE YOU TO BE; I CURSE YOU TO STAY!"

"NOOO!" screamed Uncle Hubert, trying to buck George, Mr. Mutton and Charlie off him with all his might.

George was clinging to his arm, terribly aware of what would happen to him should he get in the way of Uncle Hubert's magic hands.

Yvonne tossed the soils again.

"HERE YOU ARE ROOTED; HERE ETERNALLY SHALL YOU LIE!"

The spell was nearly done and the thought seemed to give Uncle Hubert more strength. He kicked Charlie in the nose and bright red blood flooded over the poor boy's pale face. He threw Mr. Mutton off him then slammed him into a wall with his magic. Mr. Mutton slid down the wall and lay crumpled on the ground.

"DAD!" George and Maggie yelled in unison, rushing to help their father up, unwittingly leaving Yvonne all alone.

With a great howl of rage, Uncle Hubert launched himself at his niece. Yvonne's ear-splitting scream seemed to awaken Miss Roland.

"YOU WILL NOT HURT THE CHILDREN!" She yelled in fury, jumping in front of Yvonne and taking the hit full force.

"Yvonne, finish the spell!" Charlie yelled, holding his shattered nose.

Yvonne pulled herself together and tossed the potted plant's soil for the last time.

"MY WILL BE DONE!"

Nobody moved. Everyone held their breath, as they watched Uncle Hubert's horrified face.

He's very red in the face, George thought to himself. But then he noticed that the potted plant was glowing red too. The plant and Uncle Hubert grew more vibrant until both reached the color of burning, fire engine red.

"AHHHH!" Uncle Hubert screamed, as his legs turned to red mist and were sucked into the plant.

Then it was his arms, his torso and neck. Only his head remained and, as it looked around frantically, it screamed;

"THE NOBLE HOUSE OF REDWIN!"

Then it too was sucked into the plant which suddenly turned back to an average green. And there he was. The great plant, Hubert Redwin.

CHAPTER 17

The End of Uncle Hubert

*E*veryone sat watching the plant for a long time hardly daring to believe that the ordeal was over. Then George stood up and slowly, very cautiously, made his way over to the plant in its bright red pot. He stared hard at the leaves and noticed that the plant was shaking.

"I don't think he knows how to talk as a plant yet." Yvonne commented, joining George.

"Let's all hope he's a slow learner," George answered, finally allowing himself to breathe a sigh of relief. "Where are Dad and Miss Roland?"

George turned around and noticed his father stirring on the floor; he sat up and held a hand to the back of his head where a large red bump had appeared.

"Him where?" Mr. Mutton asked groggily.

"Dad I think you had better lie down just now," Maggie said, gently lowering him back to the ground. "Uncle Hubert's gone; don't worry about him."

Mr. Mutton nodded and massaged his temples. Then a little groan caught everyone's attention. Miss Roland was sitting up too, but she wasn't confused like Mr. Mutton.

"Oh no! Did he get away?" She asked urgently, grabbing on to Charlie and shaking him slightly in panic.

"Miss...he's gone," Charlie said awkwardly, extracting his arm from her vice-like grip.

Miss Roland stared at everyone in shock. She swallowed thickly a couple of times and then burst into noisy tears.

"Oh, you've saved me! Thank you, thank you all!"

She sobbed and jumped up, attempting to hug everyone, when she suddenly swayed on the spot and was helped back down to the floor by Maggie, who seemed to be playing nurse for the night.

George looked over at Charlie and their eyes met. Then, suddenly, they were both laughing. Laughing so hard that tears ran down their cheeks and they bent over double trying not to fall over.

"WE DID IT!" Charlie screamed, punching the air with his fist and dancing on the spot.

George ran over and started dancing too and soon enough the two girls were there and everyone was doing a ridiculous dance of victory, laughing in shock, smiling in relief and singing with victory.

George was just about to attempt a back-flip, when a siren outside made everyone stop what they were doing. George looked questioningly at Charlie who shrugged in reply and everyone trooped down stairs to have a look at what was going on. When George stepped out of the school, the first thing he noticed was Samantha the hall monitor crying at the school's front gates, flashing ambulance lights behind her. George ran over to her and tentatively put an arm around the girl's quaking shoulders.

"Hey, Samantha, what happened? Where's your grandmother?"

For reply, Samantha pointed over to the ambulance. George could just see inside it and spotted Mildred on a bed with wheels, strapped down tightly. She was struggling against the binding and looking very angry.

"What happened?" George asked again gently.

In all the fuss over Uncle Hubert, he had forgotten all about Samantha and Mildred.

"I called the hoshpital," Samantha said shakily, covering her face with her hands. "And told them that my grandmother was crazy...she needsh help and thish was the only way I could get it for her...but now I'm all alone!"

Samantha's small frame shook with fresh sobs and George looked pleadingly at Miss Roland. He had no idea what to say; it seemed like a horrible situation to be in. Miss Roland stepped forward and pulled the girl into a gentle hug, patting her on the back.

"You did the right thing, Samantha. You're right, your grandmother does need help and it was very responsible of you to call the hospital where she can get proper treatment."

Samantha looked up at Miss Roland; her eyes were very red and swollen. "But where will I live? I'll have to go to an orphanage and leave Mount Dusk."

Miss Roland paused for a moment, staring hard at the stricken girl. "Maybe not," she said quietly, still looking hard at Samantha.

Samantha's tears slowed and a glint of hope flickered in her puffy eyes.

"Samantha...what would you say to living with me? I've never had a daughter and...well...it's up to you."

Samantha's mouth gaped open in shock and she stood still and quiet for a moment, processing the proposal. And then with a tragically brave smile on her face she hugged Miss Roland, too choked with tears of gratitude to speak.

Miss Roland clutched the girl hard. "I think we're going to get along just fine," she whispered into Samantha's ear.

XXX

After a happy half hour of celebrating Samantha's new home and Uncle Hubert's defeat on the school grounds, Miss Roland led her new charge to her home, waving happily behind her at George and the others until they were out of sight.

"Where to now?" George asked, looking at the twins and expecting to see smiles beaming back at him. But the twins weren't smiling.

"We just realized," Yvonne started slowly, "that we're orphans too."

The smile melted off George's face. He had forgotten about that. But Mr. Mutton stepped forward with a heartening idea.

"Would Rosemary look after you both?"

Charlie's mouth slowly turned up into a smile. "Hey, I bet she would!"

"We had better go and see her; she'll be worried sick! She hasn't seen us in weeks," Yvonne said.

As Yvonne passed George heading to her house, their eyes met and George found himself mesmerized by the dark brown eyes that stared back at him. He tried to look away before Charlie noticed but it was too late.

"Get a good look, mate?" he whispered, smirking as he went to follow his sister.

"Hold on!" Mr. Mutton called after them. "I had better go and tell Carol that we're all okay. Maggie, come with me; George you can go with Yvonne and Charlie."

"But, Dad," Maggie whined, "I want to stay with them...please?"

Mr. Mutton stared at Maggie for a moment then let out a small sigh and a smile.

"I guess you've proven yourself to be responsible. You kids have half an hour and then you have to come home."

Maggie did a little jig of victory and followed her brother and friends up to Willow Street. The air was cold but the wind had died down a lot after Uncle Hubert's capture. The plant Hubert was resting in Charlie's arms and was still shaking as if someone was trying to escape.

They made it to the Redwin castle and walked up to the large front doors but, before they could even knock, the doors were thrown open and a black and white figure raced at the Redwin children and threw itself upon them. Poor Rosemary was sobbing her heart out as she clutched at Charlie and Yvonne.

"Oh, I've been waiting next to that door for so long! Where have you two been? Where is your uncle? You two are going to be in such trouble when he finds you! Oh, but you're safe! Thank goodness!" Rosemary's words came out in a gush of tears and Charlie patted her kindly on the back.

"We have a lot to tell you, Rosemary. Perhaps we better go inside…"

xxx

After twenty minutes of the fastest story-telling George had ever heard, Rosemary was filled in on the main points of the Redwin and Regale mystery. Her hands shook the whole time as she stared in wonder at the two children she had helped raise since birth. When she was told about the night's events she gasped and shrieked; "You did what?!"

Yvonne hastened to settle the poor woman.

When the story was finished, Rosemary stood up and walked over to the struggling plant.

"I always knew there was something evil about him," she said quietly and then she swiftly picked up the plant and whisked it away upstairs.

When she came back a few minutes later she wore a triumphant grin. "I've put him in the haunted tower," she declared, smiling mischievously. "The farthest part of the house."

Everyone clapped and then Yvonne stepped forward towards the kindly maid.

"Rosemary, me and Charlie have a favor to ask you," she said quietly, looking nervous. "Now that we don't have a guardian...we were wondering if you could possibly look after us and, that way, we don't have to leave Mount Dusk."

Rosemary's eyes filled with tears as she looked upon the small dark girl and her brother, who was looking at the ground, not daring to look up, just in case Rosemary said no.

"It would be..." Rosemary said slowly, "my honor! I used to look after your mother when she was a child and I know she would have liked me to look after you two very much!"

Yvonne stepped forward and hugged the old lady but Charlie stayed where he was.

"Our mother was evil...she would have wanted us dead," Charlie said softly.

Rosemary clapped a hand to her mouth and gasped.

"What on earth gave you the impression that she was evil, my dear?" she asked softly, looking concerned.

Charlie looked up and there was great sadness in his eyes.

"I remember Yvonne telling Miss Roland about how our parents died for our family's honor...surely that meant she was on Uncle Hubert's side."

Yvonne looked up at Rosemary.

"Was it true?" she asked in a small voice.

Rosemary's face was suddenly filled with anger.

"HOW DARE HE DESTROY YOUR MOTHER'S MEMORY IN THAT WAY!" She thundered, the tears welling up in her eyes. "Your mother and father died in a car accident after trying to have your Uncle Hubert put away in a mental institution. I have always thought it was suspicious and now I think we can be sure that Hubert Redwin had something to do with your parents' death."

Charlie and Yvonne looked shocked and George thought that they must feel horrible thinking of how their parents died at the hands of their own uncle. But the Redwin children smiled and started cheering; their parent weren't evil after all! And knowing it filled them with relief. Now they could think of their parents as the loving human beings they had so wanted to believe in.

After another five minutes of hugging and celebrating, it was time for George and Maggie to head for home. Walking to their house, George put an arm around his little sister.

"You were great tonight, Maggie," he said, giving her a quick squeeze.

"Thanks," Maggie replied, smiling. "But I already knew that."

Mrs. Mutton swooped on her children as they entered the house. Her tears were all over their faces and they squirmed to escape the tight clutch of the hysterical woman.

"Thought you were all injured or worse...took forever...worried sick...couldn't sleep. Oh, my beautiful children!"

George made his mother a cup of tea and sat her down on the chair.

"Your father's told me what happened," she sniffed, sipping on her sweet tea. "You two were very brave and all, but you must promise to never get involved in anything like this ever again."

George and Maggie looked at each other and burst out laughing. Living in a town like Mount Dusk, how could they ever avoid it?

After many more hugs and a few big yawns, the two Mutton children went to bed and fell asleep almost instantly.

CHAPTER 18

Birthday

A week after Uncle Hubert's defeat it was time to celebrate George's eleventh birthday. They were having a small party in the Muttons' backyard where Mrs. Mutton had laid out a great lunch of roast chicken and potato salad and as many goodies as anyone could wish for. George's parents had given George a puppy for his birthday and Maggie had made it a new collar out of wool from Mrs. Mutton's knitting bag. George was thrilled with the little golden retriever and named him Thomas. When George had gotten home the night of the confrontation with Uncle Hubert he had expected to see Thomas Regale in the window portraits but now they were just normal windows. George had felt sad that he would never again speak to the Regales but knew it meant that they were free.

There was a knock on the door and Yvonne and Charlie walked in, both with presents clutched to their chests.

"Woo hoo!" George cried and opened the gifts at once.

From Charlie he had gotten a scary movie and a box of

chocolates, and from Yvonne he received a hand-held video game.

"Thanks!" George cried, slapping Charlie on the back. Suddenly Yvonne leapt forward and planted a big kiss on his cheek.

"Happy Birthday, George," she said, smiling, and then wandering off to find Maggie.

George stared after her in shock with his cheeks glowing bright red.

"You have no idea what you're getting yourself into, my friend," Charlie said, shaking his head.

The lunch had almost begun when another knock sounded on the door. It was Samantha but she didn't look like herself at all. Her braces were gone and her hair was cut nicely; she wore a pretty green dress and a small awkward smile.

"Sorry...I didn't know if I was allowed to come or not, but Patricia said I should."

George beamed at the girl, glad to see that she was finally being taken care of.

"Come in!" George cried and grabbed at the present she held before her. It was a potted plant. George stared at her, confused, and she laughed.

"It's the plant Patricia kept in her classroom that used to have one of the Regales in it. She thought you might like to keep it as a memento."

George grinned. "It's perfect!" he cried happily. "Come outside and have something to eat."

The afternoon went past with lots of fun. Everyone enjoyed playing with Thomas the dog and eating as much as they possibly could. George was still grinning stupidly, thinking about the kiss Yvonne had planted on his cheek, and took every opportunity to stand next to her. Unfortunately, this seemed to make her uncomfortable and she kept shooting uneasy glances at Maggie, who would burst out laughing whenever this happened.

"So," Charlie said, managing to squeeze in between George

and Yvonne. "What are we going to do now?" he asked, smiling broadly.

"What do you mean?" George replied, looking uncertainly at his friend.

"Well...now that the Regales are free, what are we going to do with ourselves?"

George thought for a moment. "We're going to listen in history class next term."

Charlie's face looked disgusted. "Why on earth would we do something like that?"

"To find out about any other mysteries this town has been hiding...I have a feeling that this town is full of them."

Charlie smiled slyly at his friend. "Well we do still have our history book *The Mysterious Mount Dusk*...feel like doing some homework tonight?"

George clapped Charlie on the back. "You know me too well," he said.

Acknowledgements

I would like to firstly thank my lovely family who have all helped me in their own individual ways. My amazing mother Lisa and my step-father Bill, both of you have helped me in so many ways while I wrote this book that I cannot say enough to praise and thank you both.

My wonderful father Andrew for his endless support of me and enthusiasm for my work, thank you so much. Many thanks to my sister Bina, who has been my last-minute-advice councilor and ideas master. Thank you to my sister Tushyana who is always so full of enthusiasm for my writing and is always there with encouraging words. My sister Emalee who makes me laugh and take life a little less seriously with a big hug, loud joke and lovely smile, thank you.

I certainly need to make mention of two young women who have been a continuous support and joy to me. Thank you to Kristy Capper, for always being there to help and to make me smile when I most needed it. You've always been there with me no matter what I'm doing and I can only say that it has made me want you to be there for all of my future mad doings. Thank you so much to Amanda Doelle for always being able to get me excited about things no matter how down I might get. Both of these women have made time for me whenever I've needed them and have added such valuable happiness to my life, my family and my writing.

And of course, thank you to *Mystery on Mount Dusk*'s biggest fan, Tommi. The inspiration for both George and Charlie, the inspiration for adventure, friendship and family. Thank you my lovely child for being such a joy to me, I simply cannot thank you enough for being who you are.

Turn the page to read an excerpt from Chapter 1 of *Mystery in Stormy Valley*, the next book in the Mount Dusk Mysteries series by Aleah Taylor.

Mystery in Stormy Valley

Chapter 1

George was just about to let out another torrent of complaints when Mr. Mutton leaned over his shoulder and faced everyone with an enormous grin, pointing out the front window of the van.

"There she is! Stormy Valley, our summer holiday destination!"

The children all pushed their faces eagerly against the van windows and strained to see the distant group of buildings in front of them. Beside the van the fields dropped way and there were cliffs with a massive heaving ocean thrashing beyond them. The grey water swirled underneath a grey sky and a sudden smell of ocean washed through the van. The buildings were getting closer and George felt a surge of relief as he contemplated leaving the vehicle for a walk on the beach. He was getting truly excited until up ahead he saw a single person standing at a dilapidated bus stop and remembered Laurence. Laurence was George's older cousin; he was thirteen and an absolutely insufferable know-it-all. Mrs. Mutton had insisted that they invite her sister's son on holiday with them and so George had to resign himself to eight weeks of Laurence. The worst part was that he was the only Mutton to not like Laurence, everyone else thought that he was so smart and sophisticated, a bright boy from a big city. But George thought he knew the truth, which was that Laurence thought he was better than everybody else and he wasn't afraid to let George know it.

The van slowed to a stop and Laurence opened the van

door, poking his brown-haired head into the packed interior. He found his seat which was backwards, facing all of the children, and gave a warm smile to everyone.

"Hello everyone, thank you ever so much for picking me up."

George fought the urge to stick his tongue out and sighed. "Laurence, this is Charlie and Yvonne Redwin."

The Redwin twins smiled and greeted Laurence. George could see a dawning interest in his best friend Charlie's eyes and wanted desperately to assure his friend that his cousin was secretly evil under his cultured exterior.

"George, how are you? You look exactly the same as last time I saw you. Funny, I thought you would have grown a bit since then."

George looked around to see someone, anyone, appear outraged that George was being spoken to so rudely but everyone was looking happily out the van windows and talking amongst themselves. So George just leveled a glare at Laurence as his older cousin grinned back confidently.

The buildings of Stormy Valley were much closer and George could see that it must be an old place as the buildings all had the crumpled look that all old buildings have. He shoved Charlie aside to get a better look out the window and sucked in a sudden breath of shock. On all of the buildings were hideous drawings of grotesque monsters. Mr. Mutton and Maggie gasped and the twin boys Ben and Bob started to wail loudly as the van passed the first house.

"What is it?" Mrs. Mutton asked in concern.

"The buildings! They've all been defaced!" Mr. Mutton gasped, still gaping.

George looked closely at the drawing closest to him; it was of an enormous horned beast with wide eyes and a drooling mouth that hosted large pointed teeth.

"What do you mean? The buildings look perfectly fine!" Mrs. Mutton said, looking around her wildly.

"No, Mum, I see them too!" Maggie squealed. "They're everywhere, these monster things."

"I see nothing either, Aunty," Laurence commented, "is this a joke?"

"No it's not a joke, why would we joke about something like this? There are monsters on every inch of every wall and roof! Who can't see them?" George asked looking around at everyone.

Charlie, Yvonne, Laurence, and Mrs. Mutton all raised their hands; they couldn't see the hideous monsters all around them. Maggie was shaking and George put his arm around her protectively. George's mind worked furiously as he tried to figure out what was happening, but Mrs. Mutton interrupted him with a sever look.

"George, this is a holiday, don't you go investigating another mystery! I want you to leave this alone!"

George nodded but disagreed completely in his mind. He would investigate as soon as was humanly possible. He would find out what the drawings meant. He looked up at them again and shuddered, they were creatures of his worst nightmares.

Other books you may enjoy from Book Rats and Neverland Publishing

Georgie Green Takes Flight
by Jen Lindgren-Brown

Somewhere Down the Line: The Legend of Boomer Jack by Timothy Martin

Longfield's Longshot by A.M. Edwards

Red Dirt Rocker by Jody French

and many more to come!

Made in the USA
Lexington, KY
27 September 2015